This book

First published 1989 by
Poolbeg Press Ltd.
Knocksedan House,
Swords, Co. Dublin, Ireland.

This book is published with the assistance of
The Arts Council/An Chomhairle Ealaíon, Ireland.

ISBN 1 85371 045 8

Cover design by Robert Ballagh
Illustrated by Robert Ballagh
Typeset by Print-Forme,
62 Santry Close, Dublin 9.
Printed by The Guernsey Press Ltd.,
Vale, Guernsey, Channel Islands.

Where is Joe?

Tony Hickey

Children's
POOLBEG

The Organiser

Contents

Sean of the Mountains

Maggie

Chapter 1

The Journey to the Bungalow

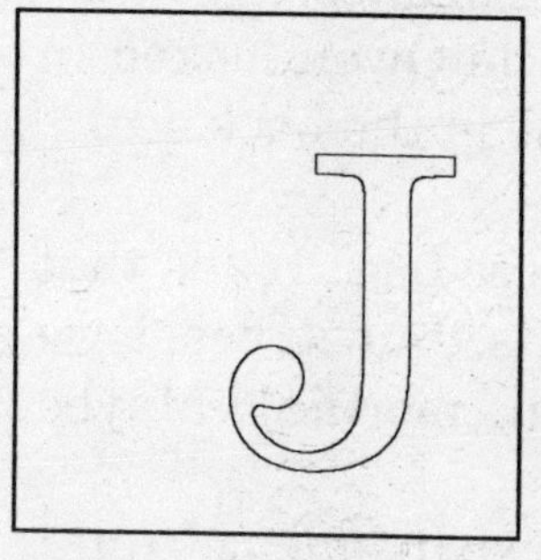

oe felt as though there was a tight band around his head, making it difficult for him to keep his eyes open. If it hadn't been for the potholes in the road, he might have been unable to prevent them closing. And how would that look to his uncle and aunt? They might think he had fallen asleep and that he cared nothing about the risk they were taking by having him to stay with them.

"Uncle Owen and Aunt Patricia." He repeated the names softly to himself in the hope this might make him feel better.

Four days ago he hadn't even known of their existence or about their children, Bart and Kitty.

Four days ago, he hadn't been sure who he himself was; "Joe-in-the-Middle" trapped between two worlds and not belonging in either of them. But maybe that would change now.

The car hit the deepest pothole so far, making its three occupants bounce.

"Are you all right?" Uncle Owen looked in the rear-view mirror at Joe in the back seat.

"Yes, I'm fine."

"So many trucks use these back roads that the surfaces get cut to bits. But at least we have them to ourselves this morning! Maybe that's a good omen."

"Maybe Joe doesn't believe in omens." Aunt Patricia turned and smiled at Joe. She was very pretty with brown eyes and dark hair streaked with grey.

"Maggie said that I had the gift to see how patterns work," Joe said.

"Oh, and what made her say that?"

"Ned and I went to see her. She tried to warn him."

"But he wouldn't listen to her?" Aunt Patricia sighed and turned away. "He was always the same, your father, too stubborn for his own good."

Joe wanted to say, "I think he's changed now," but that could lead to more questions and he just felt too rotten for long explanations.

Aunt Patricia and Uncle Owen

He tried to distract himself again, this time by looking out the window.

The February countryside was a tangle of yellow gorse bushes and clumps of trees. Ivy grew everywhere; on walls, hedges, farm buildings. There were no people and very few animals apart from an occasional herd of cows and a few weather-stained sheep.

The small towns they passed through had the same desolate feeling but, then, it was only seven o'clock in the morning.

"We are coming to Tullamore now," Uncle Owen said. "Have a good look at it in case anyone asks what you thought of it."

Joe tried to read the names on some of the buildings.

"The bus from Dublin comes into the railway station yard. We'd better show you that as well." Uncle Owen drove to where the line of railway buildings was.

Joe said, "The bus must leave Dublin very early to get here by this time."

"We never thought of that." Owen got out of the car and read the timetable pasted to a notice board. "The first bus from Dublin isn't due until ten fifteen."

"That's three hours away," Aunt Patricia said. "We can't hang around for three hours.

You have your work. And Kitty and Bart have to go to school."

"I suppose we'll just have to make something up," Owen said.

"One lie always leads to another. We will just say that we brought Joe from Tullamore and let people assume that he came from Dublin on the bus or the train. I'm sure Joe knows how important it is that we don't arouse anyone's suspicions." She looked at her nephew again and touched his forehead. "Are you feeling O.K.? You look a bit flushed."

"I'll be all right when I get out of the car."

"And that'll be as soon as possible," Owen declared. "There's nothing to be gained now by delaying." He drove out of the station yard, away from the town.

They'd gone less than two miles down the road when Joe sensed a sudden tension in the car. He sat up and there, clearly visible through the windscreen, was the cause of the change. A row of shiny caravans was parked on the side of the road. The site was much neater and tidier than the camp where Maggie lived but there was no mistaking the look of the children tumbling out into the morning. They were tinker children. Two of them dashed across the road.

The road was icy and the car skidded slightly to avoid them.

A woman appeared at the door of one of the caravans.

Joe quickly turned his head away but he knew that the woman had seen him.

Owen said, "Stupid children."

"Well at least there was no harm done." Aunt Patricia was trying to sound cheerful but Joe wondered if the sight of the tinker children hadn't brought all kinds of memories back, memories of when she and his mother had been tinkers, living on the side of the road.

Tullamore was soon far behind them. They drove through more countryside where the roads were wider and had far fewer potholes.

"Won't be long now," Owen said.

Ahead was a stretch of river lined with tall grasses, blackened by winter. An old castle balanced on an outcrop of rocks. Nearby were even older buildings.

"What's the place called?"

"Clonmacnoise," Aunt Patricia said.

The road twisted and rose steeply, shutting the buildings from view.

"Out there is the bog."

Joe looked through the other window and

saw a great stretch of flat brown land dotted with clumps of heather.

"And this is our place."

They drove over a cattle grid, designed to keep livestock from straying on or off the land. A sign said, "Owen Murphy, Builder." Surrounded by a windbreak of trees was a long bungalow.

"It looks huge," Joe said.

"When you're in the building trade you have to let people see what you can do. But, apart from that, your aunt and myself had enough of bed-sitters and small flats in England."

A boy and a girl, dressed in jeans and thick-knit sweaters, came out to the car.

Aunt Patricia said, "Joe, I want you to meet your cousins, Kitty and Bart."

The three young people stared at each other with a mixture of friendliness and curiosity.

"Let's get in out of the cold," Owen said. "I'm more than ready for my breakfast."

"I'm sure we all are," Aunt Patricia said. "Kitty and Bart can show Joe where his bedroom and the bathroom are. Maybe, Bart, you would lend him some clean clothes, that is if Joe doesn't mind wearing borrowed clothes."

Joe managed a smile. "The clothes I'm wearing now don't belong to me either."

Kitty

Bart

"Time enough for explanations later on," Owen said. "I'll go and milk the cow and have at least that much done."

"She's already milked," Bart said.

"Good lad."

"And the breakfast is almost ready as well," said Kitty.

"Having your cousin here seems to be having a good effect on you! Long may it last!" Aunt Patricia said.

The bungalow was beautifully warm with a long carpeted corridor.

"This is your room here," Bart said.

It was a fine bright room overlooking the river with just a glimpse of the roofs of Clonmacnoise.

"What's Clonmacnoise?" asked Joe.

"It's a very famous monastic settlement. Monks used to live there," Bart said. "We can go and have a look at it tomorrow if you like. We'll be on mid-term break from school."

"That'd be great. What's the name of that river?"

"It's the river Shannon, the longest river in the British Isles, but then maybe you don't learn about Irish rivers in England."

"I'm not very good at geography," Joe said, "and I never saw a proper river until I came to

Ireland."

"Did you ever hear of us when you were in England?" Kitty asked.

Joe shook his head. "Did you ever hear of me?"

"Not until that man, Pat, came last night with a letter. Who is he?"

"A friend of mine and of Ned. Ned is my father."

"We'd heard of him all right and of your mother as well. Mammy and Daddy often wondered what happened to them. It seems so strange that Mammy just lost touch like that with her only sister. It was only when she read the letter last night that she knew that she'd died. That must have been terrible for you."

"I was only four when it happened. I don't really remember her, just a kind of lullaby she used to sing to me. I didn't even know she was Irish until Ned took me away from the Institute a few days ago."

"The Institute?" Bart said. "That sounds like an orphanage."

Aunt Patricia called from the kitchen. "What's keeping you three? Has Joe even started to wash yet?"

Kitty called back, "He'll only be a few seconds." Then she said to Joe, "Was it really an orphanage?"

"No, not exactly, but there were some orphans there like my best friend, Charlie Morris. Mainly it was for children whose parents couldn't look after them. Ned is a musician and has to travel a lot."

"A musician?" His cousins were clearly impressed.

"Yes. He plays the guitar. But now I don't want to get on the wrong side of your mother by making everyone late."

Bart said, "She doesn't really have a wrong side but, all the same, maybe you should use the bathroom. I'll fetch you a clean towel."

Twelve hours ago, Joe had stood in a different bathroom. That had been in the Mulligans' house in Joyce Gardens. That bathroom had been as warm and cosy, especially after the cold, rainswept Dublin streets.

Where were all the people he'd met over the last two days? Brigid? Maggie? Jacko? The Organiser?

Suddenly there were so many thoughts swirling around in Joe's head that he felt he couldn't cope. Then the warm water and the scented soap lather on his face and hands made him calmer. He dried himself and went back to his room.

There were jeans and a clean shirt on the bed. How wonderful it would be not to have to change his clothes, just to lie down! But the others were waiting for him in the kitchen.

"Take the chair closest to the Aga," Aunt Patricia said. "We usually have porridge on a morning like this. Would you like some?"

"Yes, please."

The porridge was lovely, served with warm milk and brown sugar, and to judge by the speed at which all the bowls were emptied, the others enjoyed it just as much as Joe.

Uncle Owen said, "There's no-one to beat your aunt when it comes to making porridge."

"I made it this morning," Bart said, "while Kitty was baking the bread."

"The two of you can cook?" Joe asked.

"Simple things," Kitty said, "like stew and bread and porridge. Have you never tried?"

"We were never allowed into the kitchen."

"Who is this 'we'?" Aunt Patricia cut the still-warm bread.

"Joe was in a kind of home for boys," Bart explained. "He was telling us about it when you called us."

"I see." Aunt Patricia passed around slices of bread. "Well, as your father has said, explanations will have to wait until later if you aren't all going to be late for work and school. Now I want you and Kitty to promise me that you won't say a word about Joe at school today." "Did you remember to make sandwiches for your lunch?"

"We did. They're in our bags." Kitty swallowed the last drop of tea. " 'Bye, Joe. See you later on."

"We're glad you're here," Bart said.

Before Joe had time to reply, his cousins were gone.

"I'd best be off too," Owen said.

Aunt Patricia and Joe listened to the car drive away. "Your uncle is doing some building for a local farmer."

"He must be good at his job. The bungalow is lovely."

Aunt Patricia nodded. "Yes, he's very good. How old are you, Joe?"

"I'll be twelve soon now."

"Twelve and we know almost nothing about you! Still we've all the time that we need and I just want you to know that it means more than I can say to have you, my only sister's only child, here with us." Her eyes glistened with tears. "But still if I don't get on with my work, I'll never get finished." She began to wash up very noisily. "You'll find plenty of books in the front room if you like reading."

"Is there a map?"

"Yes, there is, in the cupboard under the bookshelves. But what do you want with a map?"

"So that I can see exactly where I am."

Joe spread the map flat on the floor. He easily found Tullamore and the road to Clonmacnoise which was marked with a cross to show how important a place it was. The name of the county on the opposite side of the river from Clonmacnoise caught his eye. It was Galway, where his mother had been born. He might even be able to see it from the window.

"You found the map then?" Aunt Patricia's voice made him jump.

"Yes. I didn't know we were so close to Galway."

"You know about Galway then?"

"Maggie told Ned and me that you and my mother used to live there."

"Yes, until our parents, your grandparents, died from pneumonia. That's when we took ourselves off to England."

"How much do Kitty and Bart know about Galway?"

"You're asking if they know that I was once a tinker? No, they don't. Your uncle and I hoped that was all in the past."

"Have I spoiled things by coming here?"

"No, no, of course you haven't. I meant what I said about how much it means to have you staying with us."

"All the same, I've reminded you of a lot of things. You got a fright this morning when the children ran out in front of the car in case anyone recognised you. I was afraid someone might recognise me too. A lot of people saw me in Dublin yesterday with Jacko and some of them are bound to have seen my picture in the newspapers and read that the guards were looking for me ..." His words began to trail away.

"Joe, are you all right?"

"I'm not sure." His headache was back worse than ever.

"You're as white as a sheet. Maybe you should ..."

But Joe never heard what his aunt thought he should do as the ground seemed to collapse beneath him.

Chapter 2

Jacko in Carroll's Bridge

rigid O'Donoghue hurried back to the camp. In one hand, she had a bag of shopping, in the other a newspaper.

She'd been nervous about going into Carroll's Bridge. After all, it was less than twelve hours since the attack on the camp. But the people in the shops had gone out of their way to be nice to her, as if to let her know that they did not approve of what happened the night before.

It was all the fault of Sean-of-the-Mountains and Maisie his sister. Maisie had stirred the townspeople up while Sean had tried to double-cross everyone from the gang of bullies. And now Sean and the dangerous Organiser were under arrest!

With the Organiser and Sean out of the way, she could now safely cut through the grounds of Oakfield House. But, as she started down the drive, she heard the sound of a car starting up at the back of the house.

Brigid dodged in among the trees and watched the car pass. It was driven by a thin, hard-faced woman, who could only be Mrs Nolan from the vegetable shop in Dublin. It must be something very important for her to drive back to Oakfield House so soon after the arrest of the Organiser and to risk being seen by the guards.

Brigid went closer to the house. It looked deserted but Brigid waited and made sure ther was no sign of life before creeping into the hall.

Three of the downstairs rooms were empty. Inside the fourth, there was a great confusion of belongings, among which Brigid recognised the green knitted hat that Sean often wore. But who had left the room in such a mess? The guards? Mrs Nolan?

Brigid ran upstairs to the room where Joe and Ned had waited. Most of the food that she had bought them was on top of the cupboard. She wondered if it would be all right for her to take the tins of soup. But if the guards came back they might notice that the tins were gone and use that as an excuse to come and ask questions at the camp. Brigid had been foolish to come into the house at all. She took a firm grip on her shopping bag and headed out of the house to where the land sloped down to the river bank.

The wind snatched at the newspaper almost tearing it from her grip. Suddenly there was no more wind. It was as though the last great gust had tired it out. It took Brigid a moment to get used to the sudden slam. Then she saw someone moving along the river bank.

Her first thought was that it was Sean-of-the-Mountsins somehow back to spy on the camp. Then she realised that the person was much smaller than Sean.

"It's Jacko!" Brigid gasped.

Her parents and old Maggie must be told without delay!

She scrambled into the next field and did not pause until she reached the edge of the camp. Dingo and the other dogs rushed forward to meet her.

Her brother, Pat, called out, "What's wrong?"

"I'll tell you later."

She found her parents seated with Maggie at the table in the old woman's caravan.

"Jacko's down by the river," Brigid said. "And I saw Mrs Nolan driving away from Oakfield."

Maggie nodded. "So they decided to show their faces after all."

"You were expecting them?"

"In a kind of way."

"Someone was looking for something in Sean's room. It was all topsy-turvy."

"How did Mrs Nolan know it was safe to go near the house?" Mrs O'Donoghue asked.

"She used Jacko, of course," Maggie replied. "She let him out of the car at the cut. He used the path by the river to get to Oakfield and make sure it was empty before Mrs Nolan drove up."

"And now he's been given Sean-of-the-Mountains' old job of keeping an eye on us," Mr O'Donoghue said. "The sooner we let him know that we won't stand for it the better." He left the table and called to his son, "Hey, Pat, leave that clearin' away for the moment. Jacko is down by the river. I think we should have a word with him."

"Right. And maybe Dingo would like to meet him as well."

At the sound of his name, Dingo fell into step with Pat, his ears alert, his tail at half-mast.

"I'm coming too," Brigid said. "Jacko knows me better than the two of you. He might talk to me."

As they reached the gap in the hedge, a growl began deep in Dingo's throat.

"We don't want to frighten the child to death," Mr O'Donoghue said.

But Brigid was already half-way across the field. Jacko had spotted the group and turned back. The most important thing was not to lose sight of him.

As he reached the bend in the river, Jacko heard a great shout. A group of pupils on their way to class had come out of St. Michael's Boarding School.

"It's a race," one of them yelled. "It's the River Liffey Tinker Marathon! Come on, the tinker boy!"

"Come on, the tinker girl!"

Jacko glanced over his shoulder. Brigid was gaining on him with every step.

If they'd only been in the city, Jacko would have had no trouble escaping but he wasn't used to soft paths and spaces without plenty of buildings.

He reached the cut and came out onto the road. There were houses on the high ground

Brigid

JACKO

on the other side. Jacko sped towards them and down a narrow passage into a dazzling world of white squares and coloured rectangles. He gulped for breath and realised that he was looking at row upon row of washing. He'd heard about this place. But from whom?

"So you lot will never learn your lesson, will you?"

Two women, one holding a baby, grabbed him.

"Where's your brother? The one who tried to steal the washing the other day?"

Jacko remembered now! Joe had been caught here too and had escaped by knocking down a clothes line. What Joe could do, Jacko could do!

Then he heard Brigid's voice, "What's going on?"

"Stealing washing, that's what's going on."

"He wasn't out to steal anything," Brigid said. "He was running away from me and my father and brother."

Mr O'Donoghue, Pat and Dingo entered the area as Brigid spoke.

Mr O'Donoghue said, "Don't be a fool, Jacko. Either you come with us or you'll end up with the guards."

Jacko didn't speak until they were back by the river. Then he said, "You've no right to hold onto me, no right at all."

"No-one will keep you against your will once you've told us what brings you to Carroll's Bridge."

"I don't have to tell you anything and you'd better not hurt me. I'll tell the Organiser. He has friends everywhere."

There was a quick exchange of glances between the O'Donoghues; glances that Jacko didn't at all care for.

Mr O'Donoghue said, "We'd better get back to the camp."

Jacko had no memory of having seen a tinker camp before and he didn't think much of the one that the O'Donoghues marched him through. At the same time, he felt proud of the way everyone stared at him and whispered about him.

An old woman beckoned from the best of the caravans. "Come on in here." From her voice, it was clear that she expected to be obeyed. Even so, he took his time, staring around the interior of the caravan, refusing a seat with a shake of his head.

"I understand that your name is Jacko," the old woman asked. "Jacko what?"

Jacko made no reply.

"He doesn't know his last name," Brigid said.

"How can that be possible?"

"He was left alone in the city. We told you about him, Maggie."

"And he managed all by himself at his age?"

"He had lots of help," Mr O'Donoghue said grimly. "He's one of the Organiser's messenger boys."

Jacko was stung into speaking. "I'm no messenger boy!"

"Then what are you?" Maggie asked.

"I'm myself and I'm not afraid of you lot!"

"But you expect us to be afraid of you, don't you?" Maggie said. "You think that because you do the Organiser's bidding, nothing can harm you! ... We're wasting our time with this lad. He's full of foolishness, just like Sean-of-the-Mountains."

Sean-of-the-Mountains full of foolishness? What kind of talk was that from people who lived miles from anywhere? Did they actually know something that left them with no fear of the Organiser?

Mrs O'Donoghue said, "Why don't you have a chat with your friend, Mrs Nolan? Ask her what's going on."

"I know what's going on."

"How could you when you don't know you own name."

"I do know my own name. It's Maguire." Jacko, too late, saw that he had been tricked into giving this information.

"I knew a lot of Maguires," Maggie said. "Were they on the road before going to Dublin?" Her voice was suddenly very kind but Jacko had no need for anyone to feel sorry for him.

He said, "I don't care whether you knew my people or not. I can get along without you and without the Organiser as well."

"I hope that's true because you may well have to manage without him."

"Maggie can tell the future," Brigid said proudly.

Jacko stared at the old woman. Could she read his thoughts as well? Maybe she was a witch.

"You're frightening him. You'll have him thinking I'm a witch!"

Jacko backed away. She *could* read his mind.

The old woman said, "Go if you want to but there's no magic here. I use my brains to find out things. I knew Joe's people. I was able to help him. Maybe I can help you too."

"I don't need help."

"You said that already but, all the same, heed my warning. Mrs Nolan is fooling you. She sent you to Oakfield to see if it was empty, didn't she? What would have happened to you if the guards had been there? Nobody gets away forever."

The conversation was finished. Jacko realised that he was expected to leave. He crunched his way across the camp to the gap in the hedge. Dingo and the dogs followed him until Pat whistled them back.

There was a sheltered spot in the hedge from which Jacko could keep an eye on the camp.

Brigid looked out the window. "He's still out there watching."

"Well, he'll not be getting anything worth reporting," Maggie said.

"Do you think Mrs Nolan is still in Carroll's Bridge then?"

"No, but he could always telephone her from the kiosk at the top of the town. He's probably arranged to meet her somewhere later on. Have a look in the newspaper. See if there's any mention of the Organiser being arrested, or of Joe."

Brigid did as she was told. “There’s no mention of either of them.”

“In that case,” her father said, “we’d better get on with fixing up the camp. We could get fresh canvas from that shop in Naas.”

Snowflakes drifted past the open door of the caravan.

“That’s all we need,” said Mrs O’Donoghue. “Snow.”

Maggie unpacked the shopping bag. “They’ll be hungry when they get back with the canvas. So will that child out in the hedge. I wish I knew exactly which of the Maguires were his parents.”

Mrs O’Donoghue smiled, “So that you could take him under your wing like a mother hen?”

Chapter 3

The Secret of Oakfield House

e's still out there," Mrs O'Donoghue said. "He must be frozen stiff."

The mid-day meal was long over. The new pieces of canvas had been used to repair the damage and make new tents.

"Should I bring him out a plate of stew?" Brigid asked.

"Yes, do," Maggie said. "Only don't do anything to frighten him."

Mrs O'Donoghue laughed. "It'd take a lot to frighten the like of Jacko." All the same, she made sure to pick the best of the meat and vegetables out of what was left in the pot and she cut an extra thick slice of bread.

"I'm not the only who's like a mother hen," Maggie said as she held the caravan door open for Brigid. "Don't trip now, girlie."

But it wasn't the possibility of tripping that

Brigid had to cope with. It was the great interest that Dingo and the other dogs showed in the food that she was carrying.

"Back off," she yelled and finally had to call out to Pat, "Will you get these brutes away from me?"

From his place in the hedge, Jacko watched Brigid with the plate of food. At first, he thought she was going to throw it away. Now he realised that the food was intended for him, that all his effort to keep out of sight had been in vain.

Brigid stepped through the gap. "Maggie cooked this. If you don't want it, throw it away over there." She pointed further along the hedge. "The dogs'll have no trouble finding it. Don't break the plate or lose the spoon. They belong to Maggie."

Once Brigid had gone, the smell of the food seemed to become even stronger. Jacko broke a piece of the bread and dipped it in the gravy and tasted it.

He looked at the bread in his hand. Then he tasted it.

There was now no way he could not eat more of the stew but he ate it quickly, turning his back so that no-one could see what he was doing.

Somehow he managed to leave a small amount to scatter in the hedge for the dogs. That would make Maggie and the O'Donoghues thing that he'd thrown all the food away. He took the empty plate and spoon back to the gap.

Brigid called out, "Maggie says you can come in and warm yourself at her stove."

Jacko shook his head.

"How long have you to wait for Mrs Nolan? It's only two o'clock now."

Four hours in this miserable place.

"Maybe I'll come in for a bit."

Brigid turned and said something to Maggie inside her caravan.

Maggie at once came to the door and waited for Jacko to get close to her before speaking. "You've got some sense, I see. But then you'd need sense if you are all on your own. Give the plate and the spoon to Brigid. She'll wash it later on."

Jacko handed over the spoon and plate and stepped inside the caravan. It was almost too warm after the hedge.

"Sit there by the window until you get used to the heat." The old woman seemed to have read his thoughts again. She was staring at him in the same fixed way as before. "You're wondering if I am going to try and harm you, aren't you? Joe and Ned wondered that as well when they first met me. I don't know why it should be that people are afraid of me. Is it because I'm so old and wrinkled, do you think?"

"No. It's the way you keep staring."

Maggie took a pair of wire-framed glasses out of her apron pocket and popped them on her nose. "There now, is that better?"

It was in fact a great improvement. Maggie now looked much less mysterious.

"I'm supposed to wear them all the time but half the time I can't find them," she continued. "Joe is very worried about you and what could happen to you. But then you don't like people worrying about you so maybe there's no point in my talking to you. But Mrs Nolan from the vegetable shop is no friend of yours any more than she is of the Organiser. Not that the Organiser was ever a friend to anyone except himself. You still don't believe me, do you?"

There was the sound of a van starting up. Jacko ran outside just in time to see it drive away from the camp in a cloud of blue smoke.

Brigid stared at him. "Now what's wrong?"

"You know well what's wrong." Jacko

pushed past Brigid and headed for the river. "Joe is in that van."

"No, he isn't." That's just Pat and Da gone to buy new blankets.

Jacko did not slow down.

"I'm going after him," Brigid said.

"You'll do no such thing until your father and Pat get back here with those new blankets," her mother said.

Maggie said, "Instead of tracking Jacko, why don't you and I go for a walk?"

"Where to?"

"To Oakfield House, only we'll do it in a nice orderly way, taking our time."

"But Jacko'll be miles away."

"He'll just find somewhere else to hide until it's time for him to go back to Dublin. That is if he does go back to Dublin."

"Why might he not do that?"

"Because he's no longer sure of himself, because he's just a child who needs to be loved and protected like all children do."

"You don't think he's gone beyond that stage then?" Mrs O'Donoghue asked.

"Would you think it possible for Brigid or any of your sons ever to get beyond that stage?"

"I hope to God that such a thing never

happens."

"Then let us say the same prayer for Jacko." Maggie took her warmest coat from the hook and then wrapped a thick shawl around her head.

Together she and Brigid set off down the road. Many parts of the ditches were filled with snow.

"We've not seen the last of that weather by any means," Maggie said.

"What is it you think you'll find in Oakfield?" Brigid asked. "The guards and Mrs Nolan have been there already."

"Yes but did the guards even know what to look for? You remember the package that Ned gave to Joe to mind?"

"The one that he collected from the cottage in the mountains? The one that had the forged money in it?"

"Yes Joe left some of that money in a cannister in Sean-of-the-Mountains' room in Oakfield House. He was hoping that the Organiser and Sean would blame Mrs Nolan and realise that she no longer was on their side."

"But the guards would surely have found the cannister. It's the first place they'd look," Brigid exclaimed.

"Yes, and maybe when they found it they were satisfied. After all, apart from the room that Ned and Joe were in, the rest of the house would seem empty. But who owns the house?"

"I don't know."

"Wouldn't it be very interesting now if it should be none other than Mrs Nolan? I recall talk a good while back, talk that I didn't pay much attention to because it was of no interest to me at the time, about how Oakfield House had been sold. It was going to be torn down and something new put in its place. Nothing seemed to happen apart from Sean turning up as the caretaker."

"Maybe the new owner couldn't afford to build the new place."

"And what if money was loaned by the Organiser?"

"He probably charges them a lot of money."

"Yes, 'interest' it's called. Don't I know decent people who've been caught in ways just like this?"

Brigid could see that what Maggie had said was probably right. People did often get into trouble by borrowing money. And the Organiser would certainly show no mercy. In Dublin he had tried to make Mr and Mrs

Mulligan part of his gang by threatening their son, Eamonn.

If Mrs Nolan and her friends were caught in the Organiser's web, they would do anything to get free.

"Are we going to cut across the fields?" asked Brigid.

"No, we aren't. We are going to walk straight up to the front door."

Brigid had never heard Maggie sound so determined. "Supposing there's someone there?"

"There won't be."

"How can you be so sure?"

"Because the only one of the Dublin lot who has ever been here is Mrs Nolan and you can bet she isn't hanging around Carroll's Bridge."

"What about the owners of the pub in the town? They're part of it too."

"They're fools! They let their cottage be used as a collection place. They've brought the attention of the guards onto themselves. They'll lie low for the moment until they know what's happening." Maggie pushed the front door fully open. "Hello!" her voice echoed through the building. "Are you here, Jacko?" The old woman stepped inside. Brigid followed.

"That's Sean's room down there. The one that Ned and Joe used is at the top of the stairs."

"That's where we are going so, up to Ned's room."

"I had a quick look in there already."

"And so no doubt did the guards." Maggie started up the stairs, the bent figure, wrapped in the black shawl, like a drawing from a ghost story. The pale grey light made the house and the room even lonelier than when Brigid had been there earlier in the day.

"Does anything strike you as odd about this room?" Maggie asked.

"It's very cold."

"Apart from that."

"I don't know."

"Look at the bed."

"There's no bed clothes on it. But that could be because Ned and Joe weren't expected to stay overnight."

"Joe and Ned didn't know how long they were going to be here. Surely the first thing they'd have done was to get comfortable."

"Do you mean make the bed?"

"Yes, but where were they to get blankets?"

"Ask Sean, I suppose."

"And if Sean was keeping out of their way?"

"Go and look for blankets somewhere in the house. They'd look to see if there was bedclothes in any of the other rooms."

"Now you're thinking well again, girlie." Maggie went out to the landing and into the room next door. "And here they are."

Brigid looked over Maggie's shoulder at the pile of blankets on the rickety old bed.

"Step carefully now and bring the blankets here. Disturb the dust as little as possible."

Brigid walked on tip-toes and lifted the blankets off the bed. She got back out onto the landing without leaving a single full footprint on the floor. "Good girl," Maggie said. "Now open the blankets one by one."

In the third blanket there was a large envelope.

"See what's inside."

Brigid tore the envelope open. "It's a list of names."

"Is Mrs Nolan's name on it?"

"Yes."

"Let me have the list while you get that supermarket bag from Ned's room."

Maggie hid the list inside the folds of her shawl. When Brigid came back with the supermarket bag, Maggie folded it flat and placed it in the envelope. "If there was only some way of sealing it ..."

"I think I saw some sticky tape in Sean's room."

"Fetch it then and a brush of some kind."

"A brush?"

"For the marks you made on the floor. We want to make things look as though no-one was here."

Brigid found the tape, almost at once, in the middle of the floor and, in the fireplace, a small black brush. She hurried back to Maggie who re-sealed the envelope. They both examined it critically. It didn't look too bad. Anyone in a hurry might not notice anything wrong with it.

"Now put it back where we found it and carry the blankets back to the bed." Brigid did as she was told.

Then Maggie threw the brush to Brigid. "Sweep the dust very lightly as you come back to the door."

Once more, the old woman studied the room.

"No-one would know anyone was in there for a long time," Brigid said. "Only I don't understand why the guards or Mrs Nolan didn't search all the rooms."

"I can't speak for the guards but you maybe were the cause of Mrs Nolan not doing it. Jacko might have been on the look-out before he went down to the river and warned her you were here."

"Why do you think the list was left?"

"I suppose you could say as a kind of insurance against things going wrong."

"But who'd have left it there?"

"Sean-of-the-Mountains, of course. He's the most treacherous one of all the gang involved in this business. He's on everyone's side."

"But Sean could never type a list on his own."

"Oh, the typing came from the Organiser. He knows that Sean can't read or write. He probably told Sean to put the list in the pile of blankets weeks and weeks ago. The idea was that whoever came into this room for blankets would find the list and, keep it. Then if he was caught, everyone on the list would be questioned by the guards."

Brigid and Maggie slowly made their way down the stairs.

"There's one thing wrong with all that," Brigid said. "It means that the Organiser knew of the plan to betray whoever went to the cottage to the guards."

"Yes, indeed he did. The Organiser has been a real gangster long enough to know when people are turning against him. Doesn't he have dozens of people all over Dublin spying for him? It just takes a careless word here and there for a pattern to start. And this pattern shows a pattern of treachery. Mrs Nolan and her friends were going to betray the Organiser."

"Why didn't Sean come back last night for the list?"

"He couldn't. He was with the Organiser, but he managed to tell Mrs Nolan about the envelope only she didn't dare come down until this morning."

"What are we going to do with the list?"

"Get in touch with the solicitor that helped Ned. Maybe when Pat and your Da come back with the blankets, I'll go along with all of you to Dublin."

Chapter 4
The Past Is Explained

he afternoon seemed to last forever in spite of a special storytelling session and talk of a school outing after Easter.

But at last school was over and Kitty and Bart made quite sure to get the front seats on the bus, directly behind the driver, who said, "You two seem very anxious to get home."

Noeleen Crowe, whom neither of the Murphys liked, gave one of her horrid smiles. "Maybe their father needs them to build a cowshed."

Kitty felt Bart bristle with anger. "Don't," she whispered. "She's only trying to start a row."

And indeed Noeleen did her best, until the Murphys got off the bus, to make fun of them. Not many of the children joined in. They disliked her as much as Kitty and Bart did. She was so stuck-up, only coming on the school bus when her father was too busy to drive her. Fortunately she hadn't been on the bus that morning. Otherwise she might have picked on Kitty and Bart then as well.

As it was, she had to be satisfied by making a face at them when they waved "good-bye" to the other children.

Then, almost as though they had got out of prison, Kitty and Bart tossed their bags up in the air, whooped with joy and raced back to the bungalow.

Their father's car was parked outside.

"He's early," Kitty said.

They hurried into the kitchen. There was no-one there. The breakfast things hadn't been properly cleared away.

"Something's happened," Bart said.

They went back into the hall. The door of Joe's room opened. Their father came out. "Joe is sick," he said.

"What's the matter with him?" Kitty asked.

"He has a fever and a very high temperature."

"Can we go in and see him?"

"Yes, I suppose you can if you are very quiet. I've got to get back to my work."

The curtains were closed on the windows. Joe's face seemed to be the same colour as the pillow. There were deep dark circles under his eyes and beads of perspiration on his forehead. Kitty and Bart had never seen anyone ill before. It frightened them just as the sight of their mother, so tired and worried, frightened them. She had a face cloth with which she wiped Joe's forehead.

"He looks terrible," Kitty whispered.

"We don't really know what he's been through these last few days," her mother whispered back.

"But he is going to get better?"

"Fevers have to take their course."

"Maybe you should send for the doctor."

"Yes, maybe I should. Is your father in the kitchen?"

"No. He had to get back to that job he's doing over at the Delaneys."

"I musn't have heard the car. But still I don't suppose he'd be against the idea of calling Dr Moran. After all, we've waited almost eight hours."

Eight hours? Joe must have got sick shortly after breakfast. Why would their mother wait so long before calling the doctor?

Joe moaned and tried to speak.

"What is it? Kitty asked softly. "What is it you want?"

But Joe did not respond to her question. Instead he drifted ever deeper into his sleep. Kitty wiped a new line of perspiration off his forehead. Then she and Bart just sat and stared at him, afraid to move yet wishing there was something they could do as they listened to the murmur of their mother's voice on the telephone, then the tinkle of the receiver being replaced.

"He'll be here as quickly as possible." Mrs Murphy sat back down. "I haven't done any housework at all today."

"We can tidy the kitchen," Bart said.

"Have a look in the front room as well. It was in there that Joe collapsed."

The children carefully closed the door of Joe's room behind them but didn't speak until they were back in the kitchen.

"You wipe those things on the draining board. I'll finish clearing the table," Bart said.

"There's something very serious going on, isn't there?" Kitty took a clean dish cloth out of the drawer. "It's all part of the mystery." Then seeing the expression on her brother's face, she added, "And don't tell me I'm imagining things because I know well that you think there is a mystery. I'm sure Mammy would like a cup of tea."

Kitty filled the kettle with fresh water. "Why don't you have a look at the front room and see what has to be done in there? Mammy might want to use it to talk to Dr Moran."

The front room was much the same as always, apart from the map of Ireland spread out on the floor.

"That was quick," Kitty said when Bart came back to the kitchen.

"There was only a map of Ireland to put away. Joe must have been looking at it when he got sick. Will we bring Mammy her tea on a tray?"

"Yes. Use one of the nice cups and saucers. You could put some biscuits on a plate as well."

Their mother was delighted by the tea and by the thoughtfulness of her children. Although she wasn't at all hungry, she nibbled at a biscuit just to please them. "What about your own tea?" she asked. "Bring your cups in here if you like. I don't think it'll disturb Joe if we talk nice and quietly. There is something I want to tell you, something that your Dad and I agreed this afternoon that you have a right to know."

Kitty and Bart lost no time fetching their tea into Joe's room where they sat on the floor, their backs against the wall.

Their mother said, "I'm not sure if you are going to understand what I have to say to you. And by understand, I don't mean the words but also the reason why certain things happened as they did. Maybe I would never have told you if Joe hadn't come to stay." She passed the biscuits to the children. They each took one and waited for her to begin her story.

At last she said, "You both know that Joe's mother and I were sisters and that we went to work in England. You know as well that I met your Dad there and got married. And Joe's mother married Ned, an Englishman with all kinds of dreams about being a famous musician and travelling the world. Your Dad and I were lucky. Our dream about coming back to Ireland and buying a small farm came true but from what I've heard so far, Ned hasn't had much luck with his ambitions. Maybe he lost heart when Mary died and Joe had to be put into that institute. But it's not really Ned I want to talk to you about. It's myself and Joe's mother. Have you never wondered for example why your Dad and I settled in this part of the country?"

"We asked Dad once and he said it was because you found exactly the right size farm at a price that you could afford."

"There was a second reason as well. We didn't know anyone around here. We hoped they would just accept us as two returned emigrants and not ask questions about our past. Have you yourself never wondered why your Dad's brothers never come to visit? Why you never see your cousins from County Tipperary?"

"No, not really," Kitty said. "We supposed that they were all too busy or ... or maybe even that there had been a falling out."

"Well, it wasn't exactly a falling out," her mother said. "Your Dad's people were, of course, disappointed that we didn't come to live closer to them. But they understood that it was a question of what we could afford and that your father might do very well around here as a builder after all his experience working in England. But what they didn't understand was why your Dad and me wouldn't tell them about my family; things that they had a perfect right to know. But your Dad and I didn't feel ready to answer their questions and so a coolness developed between us."

"They must have been very serious questions," Bart said.

"Yes, they were. They were about my life in Galway. Did you never wonder about that? Why no-one from Galway ever came here?"

"We thought it was because your parents were dead. You told us there was only yourself and Joe's mother left in the family."

"But most people have friends. Did you not wonder why I seemed to know no-one from the time before I went to England?"

"I've thought about it a few times," Kitty said, "especially during the summer when other families seem to have visitors."

"Well, the reason I haven't kept in touch with the people that I knew when I was growing up was because they were itinerants, travellers, tinkers, whatever you want to call them."

"Do you mean that you knew a lot of tinkers?"

"No, Bart, I mean that myself and Joe's mother, our entire family were tinkers. We lived in a tent at the side of the road. When our parents died, we ran away to England to make a new life for ourselves. It wasn't easy learning to behave like settled people. But we managed somehow, working in factories, as helpers in kitchens, as cleaners in hospitals. We avoided all contact with the past. We avoided Irish people. Your Dad was the first person from Ireland that I spoke to for almost a year."

"You told us how he nearly killed you," Kitty said.

"Yes. He was working on an extension to the X-Ray department and dropped a brick that missed me by inches." She laughed softly at the thought. "He got the fright of his life; a worse fright than I got. But when he got over that fright, he pestered me to go dancing with him. I finally said 'Yes' just to keep him quiet. I insisted that we go to dance halls that weren't attended just by the Irish. I insisted too that Mary, Joe's mother, come with us. It was at one of those dance halls that she met Ned."

"And married him?"

"Yes, eventually, just like I married your Dad."

"But did you tell Dad about ... about ..."

"About Galway and my life there? Yes, I did. He thought at first that I was joking. In a strange way I felt myself as though it was something that I was making up."

"But Dad didn't mind?" Kitty said.

"No. Do the two of you mind?"

"No, not exactly mind," Bart said. "It's just that ..."

"It's just that it takes a bit of getting used to," his mother suggested. "I can understand that. I hope too that you understand why I haven't told you before. It wasn't exactly that I was ashamed of being a tinker. After all, I had no choice in the matter. As I've said, if Joe hadn't come to stay, I might never have felt the need to tell but now your Dad and I feel that you have a right to know in case you should hear it from someone else."

"But who else around here knows?" asked Kitty.

"No-one as far as I'm aware but that could change. I realised that sitting here with Joe. His father is in some kind of trouble with the police. Everything could be brought out into the open. Your Dad and I just want the two of you to be prepared for anything that might happen."

Bart said, "You mean that people might turn against us because of Galway?"

Before Mrs Murphy could answer, the door

bell rang.

"That'll be Dr Moran. I'll go and let him in. You'd better take the tea things back to the kitchen."

Chapter 5
Noeleen Asks Questions

en minutes passed before Dr Moran and Mrs Murphy came back out of Joe's room. They went straight into the front room where another ten minutes passed before Mrs Murphy came into the kitchen.

"Dr Moran says that there is nothing too seriously wrong with Joe as long as he takes it easy and has lots of rest. The poor child is utterly exhausted and you should see the blisters on his feet."

"He won't have to go to the hospital or anything, will he?" Kitty asked.

"No, but he does need some pills and medicine as soon as possible. Dr Moran is certain that the chemist in Moate will have them. I'll need the two of you to go and buy them."

The children nodded.

"Dr Moran can drive you in but he has another emergency call to make further on so he can't drive you back. But I'm sure you'll have no trouble getting a lift. Mrs Murphy gave Kitty ten pounds. "If it's more than that, tell them I'll pay them the rest next time that I'm in."

"What do we say if we're asked who the medicine is for?"

"Tell the truth. Say it's for your cousin. And say that you're in a hurry. But with luck you won't be asked any questions."

Their mother's wish came true. There was a new assistant in the chemist's, who showed no curiosity about the prescriptions. She just handed over the pills, the bottle of medicine and a tube of cream without saying anything except, "There you are. That'll be eight pounds seventy-five, please."

Kitty put the change in her pocket and followed Bart out into the street. A large car stopped. The window was rolled down. Mr Crowe looked out.

"I thought it was the two of you. Looking for a lift? Hop in. Kitty can sit in the back with Noeleen. I suppose you were after this week's comics. Noeleen would give me no peace until I drove her in to get hers. Do you by any chance read the same comics? If you did, maybe you could get different ones and swap like we used to do when I was a kid."

"I hate swapping things," Noeleen said. "I save my comics. And, anyway, the Murphys didn't go to Moate to buy comics. They went to get something at the Chemist. Kitty is carrying a bag just like the one Mother gets her medicine in."

Mr Crowe immediately became anxious. "Is that true? Is that true? Is there someone in the family ill? Not your mother or father, I hope ..."

"There's no-one else it could be apart from their father and mother," Noeleen said in such a rude way that Kitty and Bart expected Mr Crowe to tell her to behave.

Instead he seemed to accept the correction. "Yes, of course, you are quite right. How stupid of me. Is it a neighbour who's ill? Mrs Costello?"

"No. It's our cousin."

"What cousin?" Noeleen demanded. "I didn't know you had a cousin. You said nothing about a cousin at school today."

"We didn't talk to each other at school today." Kitty hoped that, if she could turn the conversation into an argument, it would be time for her and Bart to get out of the car before giving Noeleen any further information.

"No and you didn't talk on the bus after school either. Where does this cousin of yours come from? Is it a boy cousin or a girl cousin?"

"Guess," Kitty said.

"What a stupid thing to say!"

This time, Mr Crowe did correct Noeleen. "Hey, there now. Take it easy back there."

"Well, it was a stupid thing to say," snapped Noeleen.

"Maybe if you asked your questions in a nicer way, you'd get them answered in a way that suits you."

"I don't want Kitty Murphy to answer my questions at all. I don't care if her cousin has two heads and comes from outer space."

"That's all right then," Mr Crowe said. "If you don't care, we can just forget about Bart and Kitty's cousin until you are in a better humour, although if he did have two heads and came from outer space, I'd certainly be very interested in meeting him. He might be able to help me with my new book."

Kitty and Bart seized on the chance to change the subject. They knew that Mr Crowe could happily talk for hours about what he was writing. "Is the new book a science fiction book?" Bart asked.

"Yes, in a kind of way."

"I didn't know you wrote that kind of story," Kitty said.

"I don't as a rule. It was just that, driving close to the bog a few weeks ago, I thought I saw a light moving across it, near where I've seen the Costelloes working. It was just my imagination, of course, but all the same it set me thinking of what might happen if a creature from space landed there."

"Why would a creature from space want to land in so boring a place as the bog?" groaned Noeleen.

"The bog isn't boring," declared Kitty. "It's very interesting."

"Oh, you mean all the wild life and stuff that Mr Donegan talks about at school," said Noeleen. "That's dead boring."

"It most certainly is not," said her father. "It's highly interesting. You don't know how lucky you are to live in so special a place."

"I don't see anything special about wild flowers and grasses," said Noeleen.

"What do you find special then?" Kitty asked in as innocent a voice as possible.

"Yes. What exactly do you find interesting?" Mr Crowe asked.

Noeleen became ever more furious. "Well not wild life and your old books."

"Well of all the ungrateful ..." Mr Crowe began to splutter. "Those books are what keep you in food and clothes."

"I still think they're boring. So do Kitty and Bart, only they're too busy sucking up to you to say so."

"We've never read any of your father's books. But Dad has and he thinks they're terrific."

"Your Dad is a nice man," Mr Crowe said, "and, of course, my wife and I are both very fond of your mother. In fact, we were hoping that you might all come over to tea on Sunday."

Bart and Kitty couldn't imagine anything worse than tea at the Crowes, where Noeleen always bossed and bullied them.

"I'm not sure what's been planned for Sunday," Bart said quickly.

"Tell them to phone us," Mr Crowe said. "I'm thinking of doing something with a couple of outhouses, maybe turn them into a work area for myself. And my wife wants to talk to your mother about a patchwork quilt. Isn't the next turn yours?"

"Oh yes, but you needn't drive us all the way. Drop us here."

"Are you sure now? It's really no trouble ..."

"No, honestly."

"Well, if you're sure."

"Yes, we're sure. Thanks very much for the lift."

"Not at all. Don't forget now about tea on Sunday."

"No, we won't forget." Bart got out of the car. "Good-bye, Noeleen."

Kitty felt obliged to say "good-bye" too.

"Good-bye, Kitty dear," Noeleen said with mocking sweetness and, at the same time, pinched Kitty hard on the arm.

Kitty didn't make a sound but somehow her left foot made contact with Noeleen's ankle.

Noeleen's yelp of pain was drowned by the sound of car doors being closed.

"She kicked me," Noeleen said.

"Nonsense. It was an accident," her father said.

"No, it wasn't. And I don't see why you stick up for them."

"I'm not sticking up for anyone. They just happen to be very nice children."

"Well if they're so nice, why wouldn't they tell us about their cousin?"

"You'll be able to find out all about their cousin when they come to tea on Sunday."

* * *

Kitty's arm really hurt from the pinch. "Noeleen Crowe is the most spiteful girl in the world."

"I know," Bart agreed. "I wonder how long it'll be before her father realises that."

"I think he's starting to realise it now. Do you think we'll have to go over there on Sunday?"

"I suppose it'll depend on how Joe is. Maybe we could get out of it by offering to stay and keep him company. It's really Dad and Mam that the Crowes want to see. Dad'll be glad if he got a job out of it. So will Mam."

"Do you think the talk of the jobs was because you said Dad liked Mr Crowe's books?"

"Could be, I suppose."

They'd reached the most exposed part of the road now. The wind raged around them, dashing sleet into their faces.

"It's as though winter has suddenly come back," Kitty said.

"Yeh. Even a space ship would have trouble

landing on a night like this." Now come on, Kitty, Joe is waiting for his medicine."

Kitty ran after Bart. She felt as though she was being blown along by the wind and that, if the bungalow hadn't been there, she might have been carried right up into the sky.

Chapter 6

At The Thatched Barge

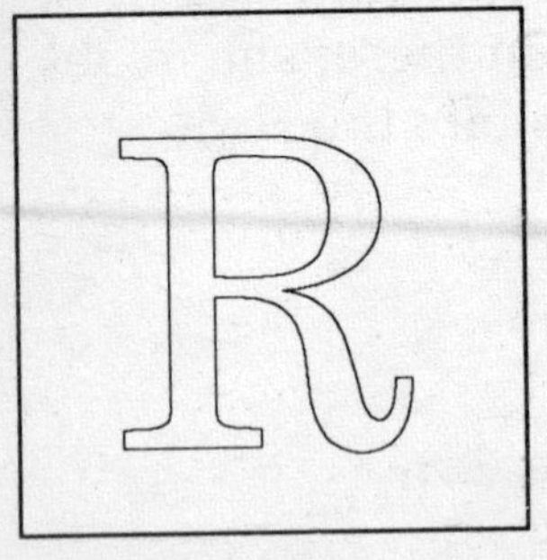

Rush hour traffic was already building up as the van with Maggie and the three O'Donoghues reached the outskirts of the city. It was almost ten years since Maggie had been in Dublin and she was amazed by the changes that had taken place. She would have found it very difficult to get to the Thatched Barge pub on her own. However, she had no difficulty at all in recognising its owner, Mr O'Neill, who at once came out from behind the counter to greet her.

"Well, well, Ma'am," he said, "If it isn't an honour and a pleasure to welcome you back to The Thatched Barge."

"We've not called at an inconvenient time?" Maggie said.

"Not at all. This is the quietest time of the

day. But even if the place was jam-packed, it could never be inconvenient to see you here. You do know," he said, to the O'Donoghues, "that it was the advice that this good woman gave me that helped me end up owner of this place."

"She read your future for you," Brigid said.

"Aye," said Maggie with a smile, "and used my head as well, for thirty-five years ago Dublin was the place to recommend to a young man ambitious to get on in the world. And you've repaid me a hundred times over since then with the kindness you've shown to me and my friends."

"And I will always try to continue doing just that. But come into the back now where we can talk privately. I assume that it is something to do with Joe and his father that has brought you so far on so cold a night."

"Yes, you are quite right there," Maggie said as she and the O'Donoghues followed Mr O'Neill into the kitchen, which Brigid noticed was as untidy as ever.

"Do you not need someone to keep an eye on the bar?" Pat asked. "I know there's no-one there now that needs serving but we might not hear a customer come in."

"No, but we can see them," Mr O'Neill said,

pointing to a looking glass set at an angle. It gave a clear view of the main entrance and most of the pub's long counter. "Now sit you down and let me get you a glass of something."

"Not for me or Pat," Mr O'Donoghue said. "The roads could be right dangerous going back. It's snowing like billy-o out there."

"Nothing for me either, thanks," said Maggie. "We'll all need to be alert. Now this is what I've come to talk to you about."

She handed the list to Mr O'Neill and explained how she had come by it.

Mr O'Neill examined the names with pursed lips. "I'd say you're right in what you are thinking. The guards would be very interested in reading this. There is the question of proof, of course, but nonetheless it's a very good starting point."

"You'll give it to the solicitor then?"

"I will but, first, I think we ought to talk to Ned and to Alf Mulligan. After all, Alf's name is on the list and he was the one who got Ned and Joe mixed up in all this!"

"Would you like me to slip around and fetch Mr Mulligan?" Brigid asked. "I remember where the house is."

"No. I'll telephone him from here. The

Mulligan house might still be watched by the Organiser's crowd. While we're waiting for him to arrive, I'll try and contact the solicitor."

Mr O'Donoghue smiled contentedly. "We'll come out on top yet."

"Don't count your chickens before they're hatched," cautioned Maggie. "Brigid, that looks like this evening's paper there on the table. See if there is anything of any interest in it."

The headlines had to do with the weather. "Heavy Snow Warning. Country Prepares for Big Freeze."

The rest of the news was of no interest to the O'Donoghues or Maggie although, as the old woman said, "The fact that it is not in the newspapers or on the television does not mean that there aren't things happening that concern us."

As if to confirm her words, Mr O'Neill came back from the telephone. "Mulligan will be right over."

"And Ned?" Maggie asked.

"He's gone."

"Gone? Gone where?"

"Neither Mulligan nor the wife knows. They were up so late last night and, with all the excitement, didn't hear the alarm clock. When they came down stairs there was a note from Ned. It just said, 'Important job to do. Don't worry. I'll be in touch soon, Ned.'"

"What the blazes could Ned be up to now?" Maggie asked.

"I hope he hasn't just run away," Brigid said.

"What makes you think he might do that?"

"There was a time when Joe didn't hear from him for over a year. Joe told me last night when we were over at the Mulligans. He didn't know whether he could rely on Ned."

"But surely with the lad just barely out of the Organiser's clutches, Ned would never desert him," her father said angrily. "That'd be too much altogether."

"There's worse news than that," Mr O'Neill said. "This time from the solicitor. The Organiser and Sean are out. The Organiser has one of the best solicitors in the country. He arranged bail. If only we had had this list earlier on, bail might have been refused."

They all looked at each other in dismay.

"No good will come from complaining about what might have been," Maggie said. "It's the here-and-now we have to concern ourselves with."

"The solicitor wants us to get the list to him without any delay. We'll have to trust Mulligan with that job but, before I hand it over, we should make a copy of it."

"Brigid is a great one at the writing," Pat said.

"Right then, Brigid. There's paper and a biro over there on the dresser. I'll clear a space here." Mr O'Neill lifted up several dirty plates, looked around for somewhere suitable to put them down and finally dumped them into the already crowded sink.

"I see you're as good as ever at the housekeeping," Maggie said drily.

"What I need is a woman like yourself to organise things for me. And maybe, when she's older, a lass like Brigid there to tend to the paper work and run messages."

"Oh aye and I suppose a strong lad like Pat to serve behind the bar and heave crates of bottles around for you. Maybe we should all come and live here."

Brigid knew that the two grown-ups were joking but she couldn't help thinking how wonderful it would be if there was even the remotest chance of such a thing happening.

"Where do you think the Organiser has

gone to?" Pat brought a serious note back into the conversation.

"I'm sure he's come back to Dublin, to talk to his cronies," Mr O'Neill said. "He'll soon realise that the guards didn't find the list. He might well go back to Oakfield for it."

"And instead, he'll find that shopping bag," Maggie said. "Brigid, I think you'd best make two copies. Don't worry about the quality of the writing."

"What is it you have in mind, Ma'am?" Mr O'Neill asked.

"I'm not sure. I only wish I was. I only wish we knew what Ned was up to because it's what he does that will affect Joe's whole future."

"Does he know where Joe is?" Brigid asked.

"No," said Maggie. "Or at least ..."

"At least what ...?"

"At least I'm assuming that he doesn't but Joe's aunt used to write to Ned and her sister. She never got a reply but that's not to say that Ned didn't receive the letters and remember the address. Could he have known that Sean and the Organiser were out on bail?"

"I know he was seeing the solicitor this morning ..." Mr O'Neill said. "That would have been after he'd left the Mulligans. I suppose the solicitor could have told him, even warned him about what had happened."

"Look up the number for Owen Murphy at Clonmacnoise," Maggie said. "There will hardly be more than one."

"You think that Ned has gone to the Murphys? All that way? He doesn't have a car," Mr O'Neill said.

"He could hire one. Look, we're only guessing when we might be finding out."

Mr O'Neill thumbed through the directory. "Here it is. Owen Murphy, Builder."

"I'll come outside with you while you dial it."

Brigid finished the first copy of the list and started on the second when her eye was caught by a reflection in the looking glass. Mr Mulligan had come into the pub. "We're in the kitchen," she called out.

"Good. I'm glad to see you're all well and safe. Who's that with Mr O'Neill in the hall?"

"That's Maggie," Mr O'Donoghue said. "They're telephoning Joe's aunt to see if they've heard from Ned."

"And I'm copying the list," Brigid said. "You can read the one I've just finished if you want to."

Maggie and Mr O'Neill came to the door of the kitchen in time to watch the expression on Mr Mulligan's face. It was not easy to tell what he was thinking.

"Your own name is there," Maggie said. "Do you know any of the others?"

"One or two people, whose kids used to knock around with my son Eamonn. I suppose the Organiser has been blackmailing them as well. Maybe they'll stand up with me now and tell all that we know."

"You'll go straight to the solicitor with the list then?"

"I will. Have no fear of that. Or were you afraid that I might destroy the list? Is that why you have Brigid making copies?"

"It's partly that because we don't know who we can or cannot trust."

"Ned and my wife and myself had a long, long talk last night. That's why the three of us were so late going to bed. We went over all that happened not just to Joe but to my son as well. We made a solemn vow that we would not in any way be part of the Organiser's plans no matter what he threatened us with."

Maggie said, "I believe you and I hope you will forgive me for doubting you."

"It's understandable that you should. After all, who knows what danger is hidden in any shadow when we are fighting the Organiser? Our own house has been watched by different people since Ned and me arrived back last night."

"They'll know you're here so," Mr O'Neill said.

"And they'll know by now that we're here as well," Maggie said, "but I don't see what we can do about that."

"We could give Mr Mulligan a lift as far as the solicitor's office," Pat said. "He'll be safe while we're all together."

"And then I could lead them a bit of a dance around the city," Mr Mulligan said. "Go to a few pubs and cafes that have no connection with Joe and Ned."

"And where do we go after we've dropped Mr Mulligan," Mr O'Donoghue asked.

"We'll make a few calls in the city. Like Mr Mulligan, we'll lead those who are following us a dance."

"What did Joe's aunt say on the phone?"

"We couldn't get through. There are telephone lines down. But we are going to try and get word to them somehow, in case Ned doesn't know that the Organiser is out and imagines it's safe to move Joe." She handed the first copy of the list to Mr O'Neill. "Keep that somewhere safe."

"I will," Mr O'Neill said.

"And I'll take the second copy with me."

Chapter 7
The Snowstorm

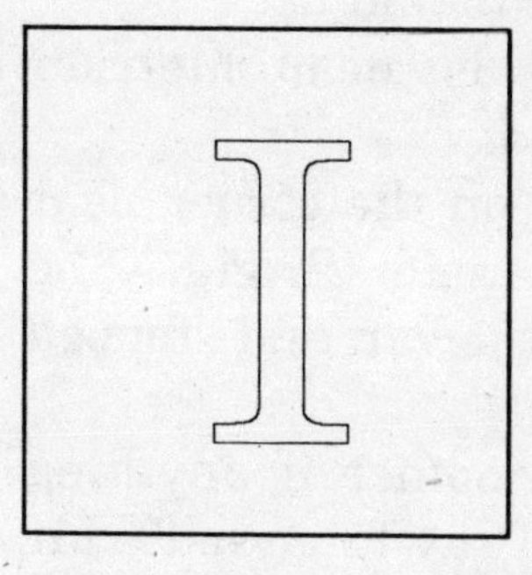

f Maggie had found it difficult to know where she was in the city a few minutes before, even the most experienced Dubliner would need to move carefully now.

Entire streets had vanished behind the falling snow. Street lights were barely visible. At every junction there was a great tangle of traffic.

"There's Mollser with the Blind Man," Pat pointed to the two people, heads lowered against the snow.

"They led us to the Organiser last night. Might they be worth following again?" Mr Mulligan asked.

"They might well be," Maggie said.

"I can do that easily," Brigid said.

"What if you get lost?" her father said. "Or

caught by whoever is following the van?"

"I won't be seen gettin' out of the van if Pat drives on the other side of that lorry."

"You won't know where to find us."

"The solicitor's office is near Merrion Square," Mr Mulligan said.

"Then I'll wait for you on the corner near the National Gallery," said Brigid. She opened the back door of the van and stepped out onto the road.

"What'll I say to her mother if anything happens to her? What'll I say to myself?" Mr O'Donoghue groaned.

"Nothing will happen to her," Maggie said. "She's a most sensible girleen."

And Brigid didn't forgot for one second to be sensible. She stood in a doorway out of sight. Then she followed on, a safe distance behind until Mollser and the Blind Man passed.

The old couple shuffled across the road and up a side street. They reached a shop. Mollser tried the handle and found it locked. She peered in through the window and apparently saw nothing. She then led the Blind Man around the side.

Brigid was just in time to see them go into a back yard.

She went as close to the gate as she dared.

She could hear the sound of angry voices.

One was a Dublin woman, younger than Mollser. "What do you mean by coming around here?"

Mollser's reply was no less harsh, "Where do you think we should go with the city crawling with guards and no safe place?"

"Well, there's no place here for you."

A hand suddenly grabbed Brigid's arm. She almost screamed with fright. "It's all right. It's only me," came the whisper.

"Jacko?"

"Yes."

"Were you following me?"

"No, I was watching to see what Mrs Nolan would do next. Did you not know that this is Mrs Nolan's shop?"

"No, I didn't."

"I think she's goin' off somewhere."

"But how did you get back from Carroll's Bridge?"

"I telephoned Mrs Nolan and told her I'd been seen. She came back for me."

"But why are you spying on her now?"

"She wouldn't let me into her house. She told me to go away just like she's tellin' Mollser and the Blind Man now. Maggie was right. No-one cares what happens to anyone but I fooled Mrs Nolan."

"How do you mean you fooled her?"

"I got on top of the shed and watched what she was at. She's packing to go away. Sean was here too."

"Sean-of-the-Mountains?"

"Yes. I heard what they were saying. She was supposed to have collected an envelope in Oakfield House. He was leppin' mad when she said she hadn't got it. You frightened her away before she had time to look properly for it."

"Maggie was right about that as well."

They heard the back door close. Then came the sound of Mollser and the Blind Man banging on it.

"They'll soon get tired of that," Jacko said. "The whole crowd ..."

"The Organiser's crowd?"

"Yeh, are in the panics. They don't know what's goin' on."

"But you do?"

"It's a list of names, isn't it, in that envelope? Mrs Nolan was furious because the Organiser made her go to the meeting last night. That's how Mollser and the Blind Man knew to come here. But quick! Mollser and the Blind Man are leaving."

Brigid and Jacko hurried away from the gate.

"Should we not maybe follow them?" Brigid asked.

"No," said Jacko. "What good are they to anyone?"

"They might know where the Organiser is. He's out on bail."

"The Organiser has no time for anyone now. Otherwise he'd have sent for us all. All he cares about is the list."

"Does that mean you're finished with him?"

"Maybe, maybe not." As quickly as he had emerged from the snow and the shadows, Jacko was gone.

Brigid listened for the sound of the tap-tap of the Blind Man's cane on the pavement, but the snow dulled any sound. There was no way of knowing which way the aged couple had gone and, as Jacko had said, it didn't really matter.

The van was waiting by the National Gallery.

"What happened?" Maggie asked.

"They went to Mrs Nolan but she wouldn't let them in. Jacko was by the gate into the backyard. He knows about the list. He says Mrs Nolan is getting ready to go away. He talked as though he wants nothing more to do with the Organiser although he won't admit it. He thinks the Organiser has let everyone down."

"How could the Organiser be so careless as to let word of the list get out?" asked Pat.

"I'd be wondering about that myself," said Maggie. "Did you never hear the old saying 'Curiosity killed the cat?' Well now supposing Sean-of-the-Mountains' curiosity got the better of him? What could be easier than for him to steam open the envelope? He might not be able to read the names but he'd recognise them as names. He didn't know what to do about the list until it was too late."

"You still have the second copy of it safe, haven't you, Maggie?" Brigid asked.

"Indeed and I have," Maggie said, "but where are we at all?"

"Coming along the canal," Pat said. "Things will be better when we get out of the city."

Pat was wrong. Things didn't get better. They got worse as wave after wave of snow swept across the great flat plain of Kildare, drifting against trees and hedges along the most exposed parts of the wide road. Several cars skidded into others. The road south was reduced to a single lane of crawling traffic.

Then, on the outskirts of Naas, there was a roadblock of patrol cars and gardai indicating that the road ahead was completely closed. One of the gardai tapped on the van. Pat opened a window.

"There's been a serious accident involving some lorries. You'll have to go into Naas. Where are you bound for?"

"Carroll's Bridge."

"They say conditions there are really bad. You might be as well to stop in Naas and see if things improve."

"Right. Thanks very much." Pat drove into the sliproad into the town. Here the confusion was just as great as traffic from the south-east joined the sudden influx of traffic from Dublin.

"It's like being a refugee," Brigid said. "You'd think we were trying to get away from a war."

Traffic finally ground to a halt at the beginning of the main street. Another guard approached the van. "You'll not get through here for several hours. We'd like you to park over there in front of the hotel. They've opened the cinema."

The old woman got stiffly out of the van and clung to Brigid as they made their way towards the cinema. They both laughed when they saw the poster for next week's film, LOST IN A STORM, with the words, "Never such action, never such dangers, never such excitement" printed under the title.

Maggie said, "If it's action, danger and excitement they want, it's to the County Kildare they ought to come."

Inside the cinema several dozen people had already gathered. Some sprawled on seats, exhausted and worried after driving through the storm. Others stood talking in front of the blank screen. The house lights were on, giving the whole place an air of unreality.

A friendly young woman approached the four tinkers. "There's some tea being made if you'd like some."

"That would be grand," Maggie said. "Maybe Brigid here could give you a hand. I'm too stiff from being in the van to be of much help to anyone."

"Then you just sit down there and take it easy. Brigid's help will be most welcome." The young woman led Brigid to one of the exits. There was a large tea urn on a trestle table, a box of biscuits and several dozen cups.

"You're well prepared," Brigid said.

"There was a big meeting in the Town Hall

last night to do with the community sports day. The cups and the urn were used for that. We thought the cinema would be more comfortable if people got really stranded. Have you come far?"

"From Dublin. We live outside Carroll's Bridge."

"You're travellers, aren't you?"

"Yes."

"I wonder if you know the other traveller who's here."

"Here in the cinema?"

"Yes. At least he looked like a traveller but then I could be mistaken. The man he was with certainly wasn't one."

"What do they look like?"

"Oh, the traveller is a little man. The other man is big ..."

"With a beard?"

"Yes. You can see them for yourself. They're still here."

Brigid went back into the main part of the cinema. Her eyes were used to the lights. Seated in the back row were two figures she hadn't noticed until now. One of them raised his hand as though in a greeting. Then he stood up and walked slowly towards her. He was exactly as Joe had described him. "You must be Brigid," he said. "And I take it that you are with Maggie and maybe your father and your brother. I imagine you know who I am. And, of course, you know Sean-of-the-Mountains as well." He glanced around expecting Sean to be by his side and was surprised to find that Sean hadn't left his seat. "Perhaps he's shy."

"Or afraid," Brigid managed to keep her voice steady but her heart was pounding.

"Afraid?" The Organiser sounded amused. "Do you mean of Maggie and the O'Donoghues?"

Maggie came slowly forward. "No, not afraid of us."

"Do you mean of me then?"

"Why should he be afraid of someone who trusts him?"

A smile crinkled the Organiser's lips. "I sense that I am involved in some kind of game of cat-and-mouse. Would you say that's true, Mr O'Donoghue?"

"Dog-and-rat might be a better name for it," Brigid's father replied.

"You being the dog? I the rat? You must be very sure of yourself to make a remark like that."

"It's not what we feel that you should worry

about," Maggie said very slowly. "It's what you yourself feel, or, maybe, even know that should concern you. It's a wise man who knows who he can trust."

The Organiser's smile hardened. "You think that you know something that I don't, do you? Well that would be foolish of *you*. I know exactly what's been happening. I know that people, who have good reason to be grateful to me, have been trying to do me harm. But since you have been good enough to warn me, let me warn you. All my friends are not in the city or even close to the city. I have friends everywhere who hear and see many things. Remember that."

He walked slowly back to his seat. Sean remained huddled inside his smart-looking overcoat, his eyes fixed on Maggie and the O'Donoghues. The Organiser stared at him and then seemed to relax into instant sleep.

"He means he knows where Joe is," Brigid said.

"That could be just a bluff," Pat answered.

"It's a chance we can't take," Maggie declared. "Ned or Pat could have been followed to Clonmacnoise. And yet there's nothing we can do here except wait."

Chapter 8

Night-time at the Bungalow

ll evening long, the wind howled around the bungalow, causing the pictures on the television to shake. Not that that really bothered the Murphys. They were too taken up with their own thoughts, and with taking turns to sit with Joe.

"How is he now?" Owen asked when his wife came back to the kitchen.

"Still sleeping, which is maybe a good sign. He really only woke up long enough to take his pills. Incidentally I told the children about Galway."

Owen looked at Bart curled up in an armchair. "What did you and Kitty make of it all?"

"I don't know," Bart said. "I just find it hard to imagine Mam living on the side of the road."

"Most people would find it hard to imagine a tinker living anywhere else," his mother replied, "which is why we've been so careful about not mentioning it all these years."

"Will you go tea at the Crowes on Sunday?"

"I forgot even to mention it to your Dad. Maybe you'd best tell him since it was you that Mr Crowe spoke to."

"He said he was thinking of converting some of the outhouses into a work area. And Mrs Crowe wants to talk to Mam about a patchwork quilt."

"I sold her one only last year," Mrs Murphy said. "Unless of course she wants it as a present for someone. And maybe we shouldn't look a gift horse in the mouth. Work is work, particularly this time of the year. Did you mention Joe being here to them?"

"We had to. Noeleen recognised the chemist's bag, said her mother's medicine came in one just like it."

"Poor Mrs Crowe."

"What is it that's wrong with her exactly?"

"A heart condition. She needs peace and quiet. That's why they left England."

Owen leaned forward and turned up the volume on the television set. Almost at once, there was a slight crackling sound. The picture disappeared off the screen. The bungalow was plunged into darkness.

"The wind must have brought a power line down," Owen said. "Hold on while I get a torch."

The light from the torch reminded Kitty and Bart of the lights on the bog. But who would be out on the bog on such a night with only a torch to show the way?"

"There are candles here somewhere." Mrs Murphy fumbled around in a drawer. "Yes, here they are. Kitty, can you manage to fetch the candlesticks out of the front room? We'll see that Joe is all right."

Owen and Mrs Murphy hurried out of the kitchen, taking the torch with them, leaving Bart and Kitty in almost total darkness. There was a great crashing sound outside. Both children jumped.

"We're being stupid," Bart said. "That's just something being blown around the yard. And power lines often come down in a gale."

"All the same you were thinking the same as I was, about the light on the bog," Kitty said.

"Mam and Dad will be waiting for the candles." Bart took four candles and a box of matches. The curtains in the front room hadn't been closed. The view of the river and the roofs of Clonmacnoise looked sinister as the wind sent clouds fleeting across the moon.

Bart put the candles in the holders and lit a match. He was surprised to see his hand tremble. If Kitty noticed, she said nothing. Maybe her hand was trembling too as she carried two of the candlesticks into the bedroom.

"Good girl," Owen said. "Put them there on the dressing table."

Mrs Murphy was kneeling down beside the bed. She almost looked as if she was praying.

The terrible thought occurred to Kitty that, if Joe was dead, the room might look exactly like this. She looked at Bart as he came into the room and knew that the same thought had occurred to him.

Then the feeling of despair passed as Joe turned slightly on his pillow and opened his eyes. He seemed almost calm as he recognised the Murphys and remembered where he was.

"Thank God," Mrs Murphy said. "The pills and medicine seem to be working already."

Joe said in a very weak voice, "I was dreaming. I thought I was in the Wicklow Mountains with Ned. I thought that the police were after us again."

"Don't try and talk now," his aunt said. "You must rest."

"No, I'm all right. I want to explain. Kitty and Bart, you want me to explain as well, don't you?"

"We do but it can wait until the morning," Kitty said.

"Just now, when I saw the candles, it reminded me of something else, of the church in Dublin and Jacko and the O'Connor children. I just hope that Jacko is safe. But then you don't know what I'm talking about, do you?" Joe tried to sit up. His aunt tried to prevent him but Owen said, "He might sleep more easily if we let him talk. It might stop his bad dreams."

"I just don't want him to get exhausted." Mrs Murphy replied.

"He'll drift off into sleep when that happens," Owen said. "I'll bet it's how the pills work. Joe, why don't you talk until you feel you don't want to talk any more? You can always finish your story tomorrow or whenever you feel up to it again."

"All right," Joe said. "It really begins last Sunday evening. I'd spent the week-end with Mr and Mrs Philips. We were all part of a scheme that was set up by Miss Carmichael, the social worker, to give the boys in the Institute a chance to see how ordinary people lived. We became great friends and, when they told me last Sunday that Mr Lawford had given his permission to have a birthday party for me, I couldn't believe it. It was the best news I'd had in ages."

"Who's Mr Lawford?" Kitty asked.

"Oh he's the head of the Institute. He and Matron run it between them. The fact that he'd given his permission for the party was very important. No-one at the Institute had ever had a birthday party all to himself. I was going to be able to invite my best mates to it. When I told Charlie Morris, who is my best friend of all, he said that maybe the Philips were thinking of adopting me. We weren't supposed to ever hope for such a thing in case it didn't happen but all the same when Charlie said it, I knew that it was really what I had been hoping for."

Pictures from that evening in the Institute began to fill Joe's mind. He could see the dark grounds around the main building, the crowded hall that he had fled from to the dormitory, the figure of Matron in her starched uniform and the way she had spoken to Charlie. "Your circumstances are quite different from those of Mathews. Arrangements for his future have to be finalised."

Joe had thought that that had meant that his father wanted to get rid of him. Instead it had meant that Ned wanted the chance to build a new life for the two of them.

"I dreamt that night of a ship on the sea and of a woman singing a lullaby." The words that Joe now spoke seemed to come of their own accord. They seemed to come straight from the pictures in his mind. As he spoke them, he seemed to move as if in a dream through all the events of the last few days. "Ned came to collect me the next day. He said he wanted to take me on a holiday. We drove along the M1. There was snow everywhere. We changed cars. I asked him why. He said it was because we'd attract less attention in a car with an Irish registration. That was the first mention he made of Ireland."

"He didn't tell the people at the Institute that he was taking you to Ireland?" Aunt Patricia asked very quietly.

"No. He was afraid they might stop him. I didn't know that I was half-Irish until then. I told him about the lullaby in my dreams. He said my mother used to sing that song. But he didn't want to talk about her. At least not for the moment."

"And maybe for the moment you've talked enough as well," suggested Owen.

"No," said Joe. "I want to tell you the rest, to make you understand."

"O.K., O.K.," Owen said. "If it'll make you feel better ..."

"I just don't want anyone saying that Ned is bad. He isn't. He was only trying to do what he thought was best for me. It was all going to be so simple. We were to go to Carroll's Bridge and wait for instructions about picking up a package. We were to take the package back to England with us."

"Only things went wrong?"

"Yes, Aunt Patricia. Ned was betrayed. When we went to a cottage up in the mountains, the guards had been tipped off. Ned helped me to escape but he was caught. Maggie had tried to warn him. But I told you that already, didn't I?"

"Yes, you did."

"I managed to get back to the camp and let Maggie know what happened. The guards had been there too, looking for me."

Joe could see the dogs rushing forward to

meet him. He could see the relief in Brigid's face when she saw that he was safe.

"Maggie and Brigid's people, the O'Donoghues, thought I would be safe in Dublin while they found out what had happened to Ned. but there was a whole plot that Ned had got involved in without realising it. There's a man called The Organiser." He looked at his listeners. They had obviously never heard of The Organiser. "He's called that because he organises people to rob and steal. He used people of all ages, even children like Jacko. But he isn't the only person who can organise things, make things happen. Some of the people that he trusted most have turned against him."

"And it was they who called the guards and told on Ned?" asked Owen.

"Yes. You see they expected someone else to be at the cottage, a Mr Mulligan, but he persuaded Ned to take on the job instead."

"In other words no-one knew who you or Ned were when you turned up in Carroll's Bridge?"

"But they know now. Mr Philips at the Institute must have discovered that Ned didn't live at the address that he gave him. He has the police in Ireland looking for me."

"And that was why the photo of you was in last evening's papers?"

"Yes."

There was silence in the room. The flickering candles reminded Joe of the oil lamp in Maggie's caravan. Her words had made him aware that he was in danger. Now his words had done the same thing to the Murphys.

"I'm sorry," he said. "Maybe Maggie shouldn't have asked you to let me come here."

"Oh, such nonsense," Aunt Patricia replied. "Where else would you go?"

"I could get you into a lot of trouble."

"We'll face that when we come to it. The main thing is for you to get well. That's right, isn't it, Owen?"

"Of course it is," her husband replied.

"Where's the Organiser now?" asked Kitty.

"The last time I saw him, he was being questioned by the guards in Carroll's Bridge about the package that I put in his car."

"The package that your father found in the cottage?"

"Yes," Joe said. "He gave it to me for safe keeping. Mr Mulligan opened it. It was full of counterfeit money."

"Do you mean that the Organiser is a forger

as well as everything else?"

Joe nodded.

"And where's Ned?"

"The guards let him go. You see, he hadn't broken into the cottage.The door was open. The people who own the place said nothing had been taken. But they were lying. They knew about the package that had been left there."

"I think The Spider might be a better name than The Organiser," Owen said. "He seems to have spun a web that stretches from Dublin right out into the Midlands and the Wicklow Mountains."

"He has an assistant, Sean-of-the-Mountains, who knows everything that goes on."

"Sean-of-the-Mountains?" Aunt Patricia said. "I knew someone of that name in Galway."

"Maggie said he used to be a traveller and that she'd sooner depend on a weasel or a stoat than on him."

"It's the same lad all right," Aunt Patricia said. "He'd bend whichever way the wind was blowing."

"I think he's on the side of both the Organiser and his enemies," Joe said.

"What you might call Sean-in-the-Middle."

Joe managed a smile. "No. I'm the one in the middle. I'm Joe-in-the-Middle."

"How do you make that out?"

"Well, I'm neither English or Irish, traveller or settled."

"You're settled here, aren't you?" His Aunt said. "And as for being neither English nor Irish, can you not be both and take the things that are best from both places?"

"I never thought of that." Joe's eyes were becoming heavy.

"No, but you may think on it now. Dream on it if you like."

"Being here is like being in a dream," Joe said.

"Well, it's a dream that won't end for a while yet," Aunt Patricia said.

But Joe didn't hear her. He was already asleep.

The Murphys gathered around the foot of the bed and looked down at him. "God help him," Owen said. "I hope he's seen the end of his troubles."

"We won't know that until we hear the end of what's happened to him these last few days," Aunt Patricia said. "But we have enough to go on with for the moment. In fact, we'll not miss the television tonight with all that we have to think and talk about. Let's all go back into the kitchen."

Back in the kitchen, they lit more candles and took up their usual places; the parents on either side of the stove, the children in the middle.

They slowly went over what Joe had told them, trying, without realising it, to put a pattern on all they had heard.

Chapter 9
Stranded with the Organiser

t's a pity they don't show the picture," Pat said. "They might as well, seein' as how the place is nearly full."

"Maybe it's a film you want on top of free shelter and six cups of strong tea," his father replied.

"I'm half inclined to slip outside to see if there's any kind of a takeaway," Pat replied.

"You'll stay where you are and that's that."

A group of teenagers had a transistor radio that played bright bouncy music that was interrupted several times by news flashes warning people not to travel.

"A bit late in the day for that," grumbled Mr O'Donoghue.

Several men, close at hand, nodded in agreement. The trouble caused by the blizzard seemed to bring people closer together. They talked to each other and helped to pass around the tea and made sure that the small children didn't hurt themselves.

"Wouldn't it be wonderful if things were like this all the time?" Maggie glanced at the Organiser, who seemed to be asleep. "Wonder what he thinks when he sees that we can all get along fine when we have to?"

"Excuse me." A neatly dressed woman approached the four tinkers. "It is Maggie from the camp, isn't it?"

"It is indeed," Maggie said. "And I recognise you. You're Mrs Breen from Carroll's Bridge. You have that grand little shop in the back street."

"I do and I just want to tell you how horrified we were to hear about what happened at the camp last night. I wouldn't want you to think that it was at all typical of the town."

"I don't think that. None of us do, but it's right good of you to take the trouble to say so. And I know that my friends, the O'Donoghues here, appreciate hearing it as well."

"Good. That's a load off my mind. Now I'd best get back to my daughter. She has three of her children with her. Oh by the way, did you hear of the other bit of excitement in Carroll's Bridge this afternoon?"

"No. We were in Dublin."

"The Murphys closed their pub up without any warning," Mrs Breen said. "An hour later a squad car with three detectives came looking for them. There's been a lot of talk in the town lately about the comings and goings at that pub. Cars arriving at all times of the day and night. That red-haired woman, Alison ..."

"Alison?" said Maggie. "If you mean who I think you mean, her name was never Alison. It's Maisie! Her brother is back there watching us like a hawk."

Mrs Breen glanced over her shoulder at Sean. "Is that whose sister she is? No-one could ever get any sense out of her. One half the town thought she'd just come to live in the Barracks. The people there thought she lived somewhere else and used the Barracks as a shortcut."

"You wouldn't know, by any chance, where this Alison took herself to?"

"She was last seen going into the pub last night. Not a trace of her since. Well, I'd best leave you now. And again, I'm delighted to have had the chance of a few words with you."

Mrs Breen moved away.

"Now then," Maggie said. "There's interesting news. The Organiser and his friends haven't been nearly as clever as they thought. If the ordinary people were getting suspicious, how far behind them would the guards be?"

"It's a wonder they didn't act sooner then," Mr O'Donoghue said.

"They needed positive proof. And Joe gave them that with the forged money he left in the Organiser's car."

"But the Organiser and Sean are as free as the wind," Pat said.

"Only if you call being stuck in a cinema in the middle of a snowstorm free. And who is to know who, apart from ourselves, is keeping an eye on them? Look around you. How could you tell who was a plain clothes detective and who wasn't?"

"You couldn't," Pat agreed.

"And the gang is scattering. The Murphys gone from the pub. Mrs Nolan packing a suitcase. Sean in a new overcoat. That list we found today'll keep the guards well and truly busy. Strange too to think that the people Joe is hiding with are called "Murphy" as well."

"Yes but there's no connection, is there?"

Brigid asked anxiously.

Maggie laughed. "Of course not, it's just another letter, a pattern of names that shows us that we must never decide that people are bad without first knowing all about them!"

"All this thinkin' is makin' me starvin'," Pat said.

"Oh all right. Go out and see if there's somewhere open. You're like a big child," Mr O'Donoghue said.

"You won't want anythin' then?"

"I didn't say that. A burger and chips."

"Just a few chips for me," said Maggie.

"I'll come with you and see what they have," Brigid announced.

The snow had eased slightly. The main street was white and sparkling under the street lights. There was no traffic and very few pedestrians.

"It's like on Christmas Eve when people are all at midnight Mass," Brigid said.

"Aye, so it is. There should be a place along here somewhere."

The takeaway counter at the cafe was crowded. The assistant gave them a quick glance and said, "There's only burgers or cod and chips. I've no time to do anything else."

"Then we'll have two burgers and chips,

one chip ..."

"And I'll have a fish and chips," Brigid said.

Brigid moved away from the counter to allow the next customer in. Sean-of-the-Mountains was watching her through the glass door. At first Brigid thought he was trying to decide whether or not to come in while they were there. But when she and Pat went outside, she realised that he was waiting to talk to them.

"What's goin' on?" he demanded.

"I thought your friend, the Organiser, could tell you that," Pat said.

"You can't turn against one of your own at a time like this," Sean said.

"One of our own? And when did you remember you were that?" Pat indicated to Brigid to move back to the cinema. "You and your sister have brought us more trouble in the last two days than we've known in all the time we've been at Carroll's Bridge."

"I couldn't help that." Sean's voice was a whine now. His face was pinched and thin with the cold. "I had to do what I was told."

"You mean you did what you thought was best for Sean-of-the-Mountains."

"I've no time to argue that with you now. I have to know what's goin' on. I saw the lot of you talkin' to that woman from Carroll's Bridge."

"She was telling us how sorry she was about the camp being attacked by that gang that your sister stirred up," Pat said.

"That wasn't my idea," Sean whimpered.

"Notin' seems to have been your idea or your fault," Pat replied. "Now this food is gettin' cold." He made as if to move on but Sean grabbed his arm and said, "If I tell you somethin' worthwhile, will you help me?"

"And what might you consider worthwhile?"

"The lad's father ..."

"Joe's father?"

"Yes. He's taken himself off to England. He was seen gettin' on a plane this afternoon. The boy wasn't with him so there is a search bein' organised to find him."

"What good will it do if you do find Joe?" Brigid demanded.

"The Organiser thinks it'll do a lot of good."

"And the so-called friends of the Organiser? What do they think?" Pat and Brigid walked quickly down the street.

Sean called after them, "I don't know what you mean."

"Let me tell you then," said Pat. "I meant

the likes of you and Mrs Nolan and the other so-called friends who are tryin' to destroy the Organiser."

Sean lurched forward, terrified. "Don't let anyone hear you say that. If the Organiser thought for a second that I wasn't to be trusted ..."

"The Organiser knows by now that you are not to be trusted. He knows that you plotted with Mrs Nolan and her friends. And do you think that the guards haven't been watchin' you as well?"

"No. Wait," Sean caught up with them. "There must be somethin' I can do, some way I can get out of this."

"You can be straight with people. You can tell the truth," Brigid said.

"Talk to the guards?" Sean's eyes stared at her in disbelief.

Pat said. "It's up to you to decide. You might not have a second chance."

Brigid and Pat went back into the cinema. Brigid handed Maggie a bag of chips and reported the conversation with Sean.

"Sean is takin' his time about comin' back," Mr O'Donoghue said.

"I don't think he was gettin' information for the Organiser," Brigid said. "I think he wanted it for himself."

The young woman who had given them the tea came to speak to them. "Are you all right?"

"Grand," Maggie said. "What's the weather doin'?"

"Oh the snow has long stopped and the wind is dying down. The roads, though, would be far too treacherous to drive on unless it was dire necessity."

"Is there a telephone anywhere?"

"There's a call box just inside the main entrance."

"Good. Thanks very much. Brigid, you come with me while I make a call." Maggie took Brigid's arm. "I'm going to ring Joe's aunt again just to make sure that everything is all right. I have the number somewhere."

The old woman fumbled in the pocket of her coat. As she did so, the copy of the list fell out of the shawl. Brigid bent quickly to pick it up. A shadow fell across her. It was the Organiser who, with a swiftness that seemed strange in a man of his build, picked up the sheet of paper and glanced at it. "So," he said, "you've been busy."

Maggie snatched the list away from him. "Yes, we have," she said.

The Organiser stepped out onto the street.

"He knows now we have the list," Brigid said.

"He knows we have a copy of the list, is what you mean. What he really wants to know is where the list itself is. And that means he'll not rest now until he gets hold of Joe."

Maggie put money in the box and dialled the number. After a few seconds, she said, "It's no good. It's still out of order."

They went back to Pat and Mr O'Donoghue. More time passed. Still Sean did not come back. Neither did the Organiser.

Chapter 10

The Next Morning

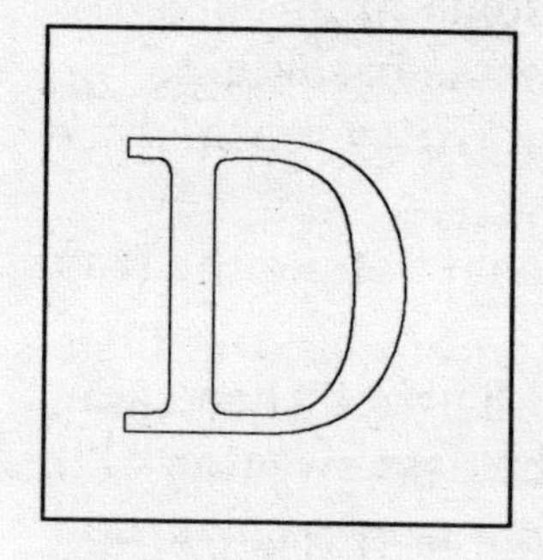uring the night, the electricity supply came back on at the bungalow On the radio, there were reports of storms sweeping the country, causing all kinds of damage. Now there was a strong possibility of snow spreading from the east.

"You two are lucky you don't have to go to school today," Aunt Patricia said, "unlike your poor old Dad, expected to work in all weather."

"You know we'd help if we could," Bart said.

"Of course you would. But even if you can't help with the building, you can get some hay to the cattle. It might even be as well to bring them into the yard in case the weather forecast is right."

"What about Joe?" Kitty said.

Aunt Patricia laughed. "Well, I don't think

he'd benefit from being left out in the yard!"

"I meant how is he feeling this morning?"

"I gave him his pills and medicine just a few seconds ago. They've done him the world of good. He said he'd like some breakfast."

"I'll bring that in to him," Kitty reached for a tray.

"No, I will," Bart made as if to take the tray from her.

"Woah there, you two." Their father came in, all muffled up in his thickest sweater. "I'll bring Joe his breakfast as soon as I've had mine."

Mrs Murphy had not been exaggerating when she said Joe felt better. A good night's sleep had made all the difference even though he was not sure if he had dreamed about talking about Ned and the Organiser. The room had been full of shadows then while now it was bright with electric light.

Owen placed the tray carefully beside him and said, "Do you think you can manage that all right?"

"I'll certainly try," Joe replied. If the porridge and brown bread was as delicious as yesterday's he'd have no trouble eating it.

"Do you feel easier in your mind after last night's talk?"

"It wasn't a dream then?"

"No. I think dreams might be more or less over for the present. Why does that notion make you smile?"

"Oh I've always been told off for day-dreaming! Ned thinks it's very bad. Maggie says it makes sense."

"It depends on how if affects your life," Owen said. "Everyone daydreams to a certain extent. The important thing is not to let daydreams ruin your life. But let's leave that for the moment. What I really want to talk to you about is England."

"England?"

"Yes. This institute you were in, for example. I think it might be a good idea if we were to let the man who runs it ..."

"Mr Lawford," said Joe.

"Mr Lawford know that you are all right. That should stop the newspapers from looking for you."

"But supposing that people find out where I am? Ned sent me here so that no-one would know. If you want to telephone anyone, telephone Mr Mulligan in Dublin. He'll know where Ned is. The Mulligans live at number twelve Joyce Gardens. The number will be in the telephone book."

"I might just have time to do that before I go out. Eat your breakfast while it's hot."

"You'll tell me what Mr Mulligan said?"

"Yes, I will, of course. Now eat."

Owen came back as Joe finished the last of his breakfast. "Good lad yourself. Your aunt will be delighted."

"What did Mr Mulligan say?"

"I couldn't get through. There's a fault on the line."

"So you won't be able to telephone Mr Lawford?"

"Not right now but I can try later on. Maybe the 'phone over at the Delaneys will be working. It's not a problem." Owen took the tray off the bed. "Will I send Bart and Kitty in?"

Joe nodded and slid back down under the covers. There was a knock on the door.

"Come in."

Kitty and Bart came quietly into the room.

"Were you here last night when I talked about Ned?"

"Yes," Kitty said. "We sat just over there. It was all a bit spooky, listening by candlelight."

"Oh, so that's why I remembered there being so many shadows. The power lines must have been down. Now there's no telephone."

"Don't worry about that. What we have to keep an eye out for is a girl called Noeleen Crowe. She knows you're here. But still maybe it'll snow and she will all have to stay indoors."

"Why do you think it's going to snow?"

"It said on the radio that it might spread westward. Co Kildare is covered in drifts."

"And Dublin?"

"Almost as bad. Are you thinking about Ned?"

"I am, but I'm thinking about Jacko too. He's got no-one to look after him."

* * * * *

At that precise moment, Jacko stirred into wakefulness and was immediately alert to his surroundings. He'd spent the night in Mrs Nolan's shed where she stored sacks of potatoes for her shop. The sacks had a faint earthy smell but they had been dry and warm and not too uncomfortable once Jacko had got used to their lumps and bumps.

He had seen Mrs Nolan sneak out the previous night just a few minutes after she'd got rid of Mollser and the Blind Man. That was how he'd known that it was safe to come back to the shed.

What would have happened if he'd asked her to take him with her?

He knew the answer to that. She'd have said "no."

Jacko thought about that for a few minutes.

He didn't often sit and think. He didn't see what good it did. It certainly didn't seem to be doing have good now. He'd be better off finding something to eat. It was a pity he didn't have a magic spell that would turn sacks of potatoes into bags of chips. He wouldn't be surprised if Maggie knew a lot of spells. He wished he could trust Maggie.

He slid down off the sacks and out into the yard. He could see in through the kitchen window, which Mrs Nolan hadn't even bothered to lock. There was the remains of a meal on the table.

Jacko lifted the bottom half of the window and slipped inside. It was grand and cosy. The food on the table was nice too, cold ham a bit curled at the edges ... But what difference? Jacko thought, as he ate a slice. There was cheese too and bread and milk. He was on top of the world.

Then the telephone rang.

Jacko ran our into the shop and looked at the instrument.

He hated the sound. It seemed to threaten his being in the shop. He just had to answer it. He lifted the receiver and, before he knew what to say, he heard Sean-of-the-Mountains speaking. "That took you long enough, so you'd better listen carefully. My sister will have a very important message for me about Joe only I don't want the Organiser to get it. She'll be by the arch near the Metal Bridge at nine o'clock this morning ... Hello? Are you still there? Are you listening to me? This is very important. Hello ..."

Jacko put the 'phone down.

* * * * *

"Hello," Sean continued to yell. "Hello. Are you there? Can you hear me?"

The farmer came to the door of the kitchen, and looked at Sean. "Are you having trouble? Did you maybe get cut off? Try the number again."

"Thanks, I will." Sean's hand trembled as he re-dialled Mrs Nolan's number. There was an engaged sound. "No luck, I'm afraid."

"Well, your breakfast is ready whenever you are."

"Oh no, thanks, I won't bother." Sean's stomach felt strange. The thought of food made him sick.

"It's all included in the price," the farmer said.

"No, I'd best be off. What do I owe you?"

"Six pounds, including the telephone calls, seeing that you didn't have any breakfast."

Sean counted out six pounds. "Thanks very much."

"Which direction are you going?"

"Oh, I've not decided yet. What I mean is that I might make it back towards the city. 'Bye. Thanks again."

The farmer and his wife watched Sean get into the Organiser's car and drive away.

"There's something very odd about that lad," the woman said. "If it hadn't been such a terrible night last night, I'd have said we didn't do bed and breakfast this time of the year."

"I made a note of the number of the car," her husband replied, "not that he'll get far with the roads in their present condition."

It took all Sean's concentration to keep the car in a straight line. The roads were like glass with the hedges on either side piled high with snow. But at least he could see the road. Last night, it had been impossible. The windscreen had kept freezing over until at last he'd been forced to admit that he could not go another yard. That was when he'd spotted the bed-and-breakfast sign and gone into the farmhouse.

The owners had obviously not been very happy to have him ask if they had a room for the night. They had barely been able to conceal their curiosity about who he was and where he was going. He'd dodged most of the questions but he was sure that they had listened when he'd contacted his sister on the 'phone. Then there was that conversation with Mrs Nolan.

But did anything matter now except the Organiser?

How long had he waited in the cinema for Sean to bring back hot food before he realised that Sean had gone and taken the car with him?

Chapter 11
Dangerous Roads

ean stayed on the back roads. That way, there was less chance of the Organiser being able to trace him. Ahead there was a cross roads with a signpost covered in snow.

He applied a little gentle pressure to the brakes. The car at once began to slip sideways.

Sean applied a little more pressure. The car seemed to straighten up. Then it went completely out of control, turning around in a circle the full width of the cross-roads.

As if from nowhere, there was a second car on the scene, and there was a great crunching of metal as the vehicles collided and swerved together like machines in a strange dance.

Sean felt as weak as a kitten as he got out of the car and glanced quickly at the second vehicle. There, seated behind the steering wheel, her hands held to her forehead, was Mrs Nolan.

Slowly, very slowly, she lowered her hands and forced herself to stop trembling. Then all sign of fear went from her face as she recognised Sean. "I thought you were the Organiser," she said as she clambered out of her car. "I thought somehow you knew where I was."

"How did you get here so quickly?" Sean demanded.

"Quickly?" Mrs Nolan said. "It's taken me all night. I had to shelter back there for hours. I thought I was going to freeze."

"But I spoke to you less than twenty minutes ago. I 'phoned you at the shop."

"You couldn't have. The place is all locked up."

"Then who answered the 'phone?"

"I don't know. Did she sound like me?"

"I didn't hear a voice. I just assumed it was you ..."

"And I suppose blurted out something."

"Yes. I spoke to my sister, Alison, before I called you."

Mrs Nolan snorted. "Alison how are you! Where did she get that name?"

"She's practising to be one of the settled people."

"If she has any sense, she'll continue travelling instead of settling down."

Sean pointed to the suitcase on the back seat of Mrs Nolan's car. "By the look of things, you're on the move yourself."

"Word is out that the Organiser is in trouble, that he has been betrayed. But then you were with him. You must know better than anyone what he's thinking."

"He's thinking just as you say. That's why I tried to telephone you this morning after I spoke to Alison. I told her to find out all that she could. I was hoping you might meet her."

"And you said this to whoever answered my 'phone?"

Sean nodded miserably. "How was I to know you'd gone?"

"All right, all right. Don't whinge."

"Where were you going to anyway?"

"I was hoping to get back to Oakfield House for the list. Is that where you were headed?" Mrs Nolan asked.

"Maybe. What were you going to do with the list?"

"Use it to make others who are on it to help me. I have to get as far away as possible.

Don't forget that I own that house. The guards will be on to me."

"Well, it doesn't look as though you are going to get very far in that car," Sean said.

"Oh I think I might just about manage to drive it," Mrs Nolan said. "I'd say you were the one who has the trouble going places."

"We could always help each other."

"Like the way you helped me get rid of the Organiser and Mr Mulligan?"

"It wasn't my fault that things went wrong. That was all due to Joe and the O'Donoghues and Maggie, bad cess to the lot of them. This time things are much simpler. The Organiser is stranded in Naas. So are the O'Donoghues and Maggie. Now give me a hand to get this car off the road."

Mrs Nolan hesitated. Then she admitted to herself that, for the moment at least, she needed Sean's help. "All right."

She steered while Sean pushed and pushed and fell down several times on the icy road. At last they guided the car into an open gate and out of sight into a field.

"We'll leave a note," Mrs Nolan said. Quickly she scribbled on a page from a notebook. "Gone for help. No-one hurt. Don't worry. Be back as soon as possible."

They got into Mrs Nolan's car, which started easily enough. "You'll have to direct me when we get closer to Carroll's Bridge. According to a signpost, I saw further back it's in this direction."

Sean nodded. "Do you think we could have the heater on?"

"It is on. Maybe it isn't working after the crash."

The heater wasn't the only thing wrong with the car. Fumes began to get in from the exhaust. The interior began to mist up. Mrs Nolan had to keep wiping the windscreen in order to see out. Then the engine began to cough and splutter and give out plumes of blue smoke.

"Will it get us there at all?" Sean demanded.

"I'm more worried about the attention we'll attract," Mrs Nolan replied. "How far are we from Carroll's Bridge, would you say?"

"Are you suggesting we walk?"

The car answered that question for them by shuddering to a halt.

Once more, Mrs Nolan steered and Sean pushed. Once more, they left a car out of sight in a field. Once more, Mrs Nolan wrote a note.

Sean didn't feel very much like smiling

when Mrs Nolan handed him her suitcase.

"I can't carry it, not in these shoes," she said.

* * * * *

It was now snowing over most of Ireland.

In the main street in Naas, drivers stretched and yawned and prepared for the journey home. The roads might not be any safer but at least they had daylight on their side.

Maggie and the O'Donoghues watched the Organiser walking around the parked cars.

Pat said, "I think Sean-of-the-Mountains has done a flit!"

"He'll not get far," Mr O'Donoghue said.

"He's been gone all night," Maggie said, "while we just sat."

"But there was nothing else we could do," Brigid pointed out. "We couldn't have got anywhere on those roads."

"Yet Sean did because he made the effort. Have we not got more cause to take risks than he had? Between us, we helped get Joe to where he is now. It's up to us to get word to him now about what's been happening," Maggie replied.

Mr O'Donoghue said. "Let's go out on the main road and see exactly what the conditions are like."

A milk lorry had overturned on the outskirts of the town, shedding its load across two lanes. A few yards on, two men were trying to start a car that had stalled. Traffic from Dublin was only a trickle of its usual flood. Traffic into the city was almost non-existent.

The same guard as the previous night was still on duty. He remembered Maggie and the others when Pat rolled down the window to speak to him. "You did the wise thing staying the night," he said. "There's been dozens of accidents between here and Kildare. They say there's more snow due this afternoon."

"And what state are the roads in further on in the direction of Tullamore or Athlone for example?" Maggie asked.

"They escaped the worst of the blizzard last night as far as I know," the guard said. "But I thought you were from Carroll's Bridge."

"We have friends down Moate way. We wondered how they might have fared."

"Better than we did here. But if you take my advice, you'll not go visiting today. Safe home to you now."

Pat drove on. "It sounds risky. We might not get there and back before it snows again. And Ma will be frantic with the worry."

"Da, could you not go to the camp and let them know that we are all right?" suggested Brigid. "You'd be more help there. Pat and I will stay with Maggie."

"You'd better make your minds up quick," Maggie said. "We're comin' to the turn-off to Carroll's Bridge. If you won't drive me, leave me here and I'll see if I can hitch-hike to Joe's aunt."

"You are a terrible woman," Mr O'Donoghue said. "You are leaving us with no choice. Drop me off just here. I'll walk back to the camp although what Brigid's mother will say I dread to think."

Yet, in spite of his worries, Mr O'Donoghue didn't blame Maggie for being determined. Joe had to be warned and protected.

He turned his collar up against the cold and remembered the last big snow in Ireland. Things had certainly improved for many of the travellers since then. He hoped they would continue to do so for the sake of Brigid and her brothers.

A car squelched to a stop next to him. It was Mrs Breen from the back street with her daughter and grandchildren. “Can we give you a lift?”

“No, thanks, Ma’am. I’m nearly home now and my boots’d only mess up the car.”

“Where did Maggie and the others go?”

“They had a message to do. I thought it best to see that everything at the camp was all right.”

Mrs Breen’s daughter nodded in the direction of a side road. “Are those some of your people there?”

Mr O’Donoghue looked at the bedraggled couple limping towards them down the road. The man carried a suitcase. Mr O’Donoghue laughed. “No, they aren’t my people but I do know who they are.”

Chapter 12

Noeleen goes Visiting

Noeleen Crowe watched the garden vanish under a cover of snow. She yawned and sighed and let the comics that she had already read three times fall onto the floor.

"Gracious me!" Mrs Grady, the house-keeper, exclaimed from the kitchen. "Such a child for noise! Can you not sit quiet for even a few minutes?"

"I've been sitting quietly ever since breakfast time," replied Noeleen.

"Which is all of fifteen minutes ago, when I arrived in the house. All you've done since then is sigh and yawn and creak around on that leather sofa until you made it sound as though there was a row boat tied up in the living room!

"Sitting room," corrected Noeleen.

"And is that not the same thing? Can you not sit in a living room? Or maybe you mean you can't live in a sitting room?"

Noeleen hated it when Mrs Grady made fun of her like that. Somehow Noeleen always ended up feeling silly and childish, yet she could not resist answering back. "It's our room and we will call it what we like."

"Oh, please yourself and feel comfortable. It's no skin off my back. But what about all the noise and the effect it might have on your poor mother?"

"She isn't poor. She's sick."

"Sick then and not likely to get better listening to you banging around the place. You know she has to get as much rest as possible. But still maybe I shouldn't pick on you for it can't be very easy for you the way things are. It's the cold weather that makes me cantankerous. It brings on my rheumatism."

"Mrs Grady and her old rheumatism," thought Noeleen. "And if it's not her rheumatism it's her sinuses."

It was amazing Mrs Grady ever felt well enough to come in and look after the house for them.

"I could do the work just as well if I wanted

to," Noeleen told herself.

But she didn't really want to even though it might give her an excuse to get out of going to school. She hated school. Lately, in fact, she hated most things; the house, the fields, the loneliness of the countryside, the steady click-click of her father's word processor. Most of all she hated the fact that her mother had to spend so much time in bed.

"You ought to make some friends," Mrs Grady said, "instead of moping around the house."

"I don't need any friends."

"Oh well now, that's where you are very wrong. Everyone needs friends. What about Bart and Kitty?"

"Their father is a builder."

"And what the blazes is wrong with being a builder?"

"He might be going to do some work for my father."

"Well, I work for your father as well and for your mother too. Does that mean that you think it beneath you to talk to me?"

Noeleen made no reply.

"Well of all the ... " Mrs Grady spluttered. "For two pins I'd go straight upstairs to your mother and hand in my notice, only I don't want to upset her with your nonsense. But I'll not say another word to you."

"That suits me fine," thought Noeleen.

Then she began to wonder how sensible that was. Mrs Grady could be very useful to her when it came to having things washed and ironed quickly. Plus her father would notice if Mrs Grady wasn't her usual chatty self. Noeleen didn't want to risk another row with him after the words they had had in the car last night over Kitty and Bart Murphy.

In fact it all came back to the Murphys for being so stuck-up about their cousin. Maybe she could get her own back on them and at the same time makeup with Mrs Grady. She said "Please, Mrs Grady, I'm sorry, and you're right, I should make friends with Kitty and Bart. I'll go over and see them right now."

Mrs Grady, who hated to be on bad terms with anyone, nodded her head. "Oh all right. I forgive you, only put on your wellingtons and lots of warm clothes. It's bitterly cold out."

"Oh I don't mind that. I like walking in the snow."

And Noeleen really did like snowy weather. She'd go along the road past the Nuns' Chapel, where Dervorgilla, whom many people blamed for the Normans coming to

Ireland, was buried. Noeleen had a great admiration for famous women. She must get Mr Donegan at school to tell them the story once more.

"Where are you off to then?" Mr Crowe had come out of his work-room in search of a match for his pipe just as Noeleen was putting on her wellingtons.

"Over to see the Murphys," Noeleen said.

"Oh good. Don't forget to find out if they are coming to tea on Sunday."

"Tea?" said Mrs Grady. "It's the first I've heard of people coming to tea. I'd better make some scones and that fruit cake that Noeleen is so fond of even though she'd rather die than say so."

Noeleen's pretence at being nice disappeared. "How do you know that I like it if I never say so?"

"Because given the chance you'd eat it until it came out of your ears. As soon as I get the casserole ready for lunch I'll start baking."

Noeleen groaned. "Not another casserole!"

"Well, no doubt but your good humour didn't last long," declared Mrs Grady. "A casserole is grand food for this weather. It's easily reheated as well for the supper. But I don't know why I'm wasting my time explaining things to you. You were only pretending to be nice."

Noeleen caught her father's eye and at once began to protest. "No, that's not true. I didn't mean to be rude. I'll be better once I've seen Kitty and Bart."

"Don't forget to ask about their cousin," Mr Crowe said.

"What cousin is that?" asked Mrs Grady. "I met Mrs Murphy in Shannonbridge on Wednesday and she said nothing about a cousin coming to stay, unless it's one of the relations from Tipperary on his half-term break."

"Wherever he's from, he's sick in bed" Mr Crowe said. "It might be nice, Noeleen, if you were to lend him some of your comics."

The telephone rang and Noeleen seized the opportunity to hide her new comics behind the sofa and take a few old ones out of the magazine rack. Her father didn't notice when he came back from answering the 'phone. "That was the book shop in Athlone," he said. "They have the book on space travel that I've been waiting for. They'll send it out this afternoon on Martin Delaney's van with the special health food for your mother."

"That's great," Noeleen said. "See you later

on." She looked into the kitchen where Mrs Grady was chopping carrots. "Bye, Mrs Grady."

" 'Bye, Noeleen. And don't cause trouble over at the Murphys.'

"Silly old thing," Noeleen thought as she started down the garden path, although there was no denying that Mrs Grady was a terrific cook and was right when she said that Noeleen would die rather than admit it.

For a moment Noeleen wished she didn't find it so hard to be nice. She just hated living here knowing that her friends were having a great time in London, or so she imagined. She hadn't heard from them for a long time. But then she hadn't written to them for ages either. They might not be her friends anymore. They might have forgotten all about her. Well, one day she'd do something that would make them all want to know her again.

She pushed a strand of hair back under her beret and began to half-walk, half-slid along the road. The snow was quite hard considering how recently it had fallen. Wouldn't it be great if the river froze like the picture in one of her mother's books about Holland where the ice was so thick that the skaters had been able to light fires on it?

She passed the new graveyard, then the white gates of a farmhouse and looked in at the Nuns' Chapel, which was separate from the main ruins of Clonmacnoise and looked very small and lonely.

In summer the whole place was different with coaches and cars from all over the place. There wouldn't be any visitors to-day. The whole area seemed deserted.

A car passed her, going in the direction of Shannonbridge. There was no friendly wave or gentle honk of the horn like the local people always gave. Not that that worried Noeleen as she came within sight of the Murphys' bungalow.

The lights were on in the hall and the front room and in another room as well which Noeleen guessed to be a bedroom.

"That must be where the sick cousin is," Noeleen thought. "Thank goodness no-one thought to close the curtains."

Quickly she climbed up on a pile of stones that would eventually form part of a rockery. She had a very clear view of the inside of the bedroom.

Kitty was sitting on the edge of the bed, Bart on a chair. They were both listening to the boy, propped up against several pillows.

"So that's the visiting cousin, is it?" Noeleen said to herself. "Well, he doesn't look all that sick to me."

She ran to the front door and rang the bell.

Several seconds passed before Mrs Murphy opened the door. "Why, hello, Noeleen! This is a surprise."

"I brought some comics for your nephew. Kitty told me he was sick."

"That's very kind of you."

"And to find out if you were coming to tea on Sunday."

"Oh dear, I'm afraid we haven't had time to discuss that yet."

"Father and Mother are looking forward to seeing you. Your nephew can come as well."

"We'll do our very best."

For a moment Noeleen thought that Mrs Murphy would just take the comics and close the door. But fortunately Mrs Murphy remembered her manners and said, "Come in for a while. You must be cold after the walk." She led the way into the kitchen. "I'll tell Kitty that you are here."

Kitty looked far from friendly when she followed her mother down the corridor. "Hello," she said very briskly.

"I brought some comics for your cousin."

Kitty took the dog-eared comics with barely a glance at them. "Thanks."

"He can have more when he's finished those. Can I come and meet him?"

"He's resting," Kitty said.

"I'll only stay a second."

"Maybe some other time," Mrs Murphy said. "Would you like a cup of tea?"

Noeleen was tempted to say "yes" just in order to annoy them but she knew she'd be wasting her time. Kitty and her mother were determined not to let her meet their visitor. "No, thanks. I said I wouldn't stay long on account of the snow."

"Of course. Tell your parents I'll let them know about tea on Sunday." Mrs Murphy saw Noeleen to the front door and let her out. "Safe home now." She felt very relieved as she went back to the kitchen.

Kitty called from the front room. "She's standing at the rockery looking at Joe's window. But she won't see anything because I closed the curtains as soon I heard her speaking to you. She only came around here to spy on us."

Noeleen left the rockery and walked to the cattle grid by the gate where she once more paused to fix her hair under her beret. The visit had not lasted long but it had been well worthwhile. Why were the Murphys so determined to stop her from meeting the strange boy? Could he have some terrible disease? But they wouldn't be in his bedroom if that was the case.

"I'll call again," Noeleen thought. "They won't expect me to do that."

A car came around the corner. It was the car that she had seen earlier on. The man who was driving looked at her. Noeleen had never seen him before. She didn't care much for the look of him. She made no attempt to wave at him before he drove past.

Chapter 13

Joe at Risk

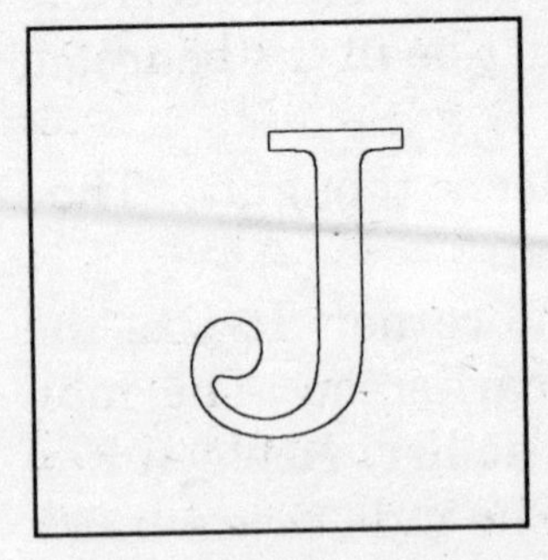

acko deliberately arrived fifteen minutes late at the arch by the Metal Bridge and had no trouble recognising Maisie, Sean's sister, by her red hair and quick, darting eyes. When he spoke to her she drew back, demanding to know who he was.

"I'm Jacko. I was at Mrs Nolan's when your brother 'phoned. You're supposed to have a message about Joe."

"Why didn't Mrs Nolan come?"

"She couldn't. Now are you going to give me the message or are you not? I'm not goin' to hang around here and maybe be picked up by the guards."

Maisie glanced fearfully along the quays. "What makes you think that the guards are interested in you?"

"The guards is interested in everyone this

morning. Now have you a message or have you not?"

"Friends of mine, the O'Sheas, seen Joe being driven through Co. Offaly early yesterday morning." She bit her lips anxiously. "Where did Sean telephone Mrs Nolan from?"

"I don't know. Where was he when you spoke to you?"

"I don't know that either. He woke me up at the crack of dawn in the boarding house that I sometimes lodge in, demanding news. He got me up out of my warm bed to go traipsin' around the city, insistin' that I find somethin' out by nine o'clock. It was just pure chance that I met the O'Sheas."

"And is that all the news that the O'Sheas had about Joe? That he's in Co. Offaly?"

"He was headin' out of Tullamore with two people, a man and a women, in a car. I have the licence number." She handed Jacko a scrap of paper. "Mrs O'Shea saw Joe in Dublin the other day and recognised him from his picture in the evening paper."

"Yes, I know," Jacko said.

"What do you mean you know?"

"I was with Joe at the time. The O'Sheas were beggin' in Nassau Street. Is there nothing else you have to tell me?"

"No, just that the O'Sheas have people on the lookout for the car, not that they'll get much driving done in this weather."

"They managed to get to Dublin, didn't they?"

"They came back yesterday before the snow."

"What brought them back so soon? Were they maybe hopin' to sell the information about Joe? Did you pay them for it?"

"And if I did what difference does that make to you? I'm just sorry I ever got mixed up in this business of Sean and ... and ... "

"And the Organiser?" said Jacko

"Oh, so you know about him as well! It seems to me that the whole world knows of him, yet people talk about him as though he was the greatest mystery imaginable."

Jacko laughed. "His secret was given away."

He laughed even more when he saw the frightened look this brought to Maisie's face and the way she began to stammer. "I hope no one thinks that I had aught to do with that. I was only helpin' my brother and now I don't even know where he is."

"I'll bet he's gone a long way away," Jacko grinned.

"Like the people from the pub in Carroll's Bridge and everyone else I ever spoke to." She was angry now, angry at being made a fool of, angry that so young a boy as Jacko was laughing at her. "You may think you're smart and clever but you're worse off than I am. I can go where I choose. I've done my last bit of dirty work. Don't try followin' me."

She walked quickly out of sight into the maze of sidestreets. Jacko would have had no trouble in following her but he knew that there was no point in doing that. Nothing would persuade her to get involved again. Jacko meanwhile was left with the key to Mrs Nolan's shop and the licence number of a car.

How could he use either of those things to the greatest benefit for himself? There had to be someone who would protect him in return for the information he'd got from Sean's sister.

* * * * *

"Are you sure we're on the right road?" Pat asked for the third time in as many minutes.

"Of course we are," Maggie said. "The quickest way to Clonmacnoise is to stay on the main road to Galway and turn off after Moate. A child of nine could tell you that."

"I'd like to see a child of nine drive along a slippery road like this!"

But then Pat felt guilty for being abrupt with the old Maggie. "I didn't mean to snap at you. There was a sign for a cafe up ahead. Why don't we stop there?"

"All right," Maggie said.

She and the two O'Donoghues had no trouble being served. The cafe was almost empty although the owner said that the roads ahead were not too bad by all accounts.

"The nearer we get to Joe the better the news," Maggie blew on her tea to cool it. "I feel better now that we've taken a bit of a break. When you get to my age any kind of disturbance can set you thinking all kinds of thoughts. Last night in that cinema, knowing that an enemy was watching, and the night before, the attack on the camp; it's all left me feeling a bit dothery."

Brigid had never heard Maggie speak like that before. "But you've always been able for everything. You stood up to that gang that attacked the camp."

"I know I did but I'm feeling tired now. Do you remember what Mr O'Neill said about me helping him run the house at the Thatched Barge?"

Brigid's heart seemed to leap."Would you even consider that idea?"

"I might," Maggie said, "when this business of Joe is over and I've decided what to do about Jacko."

"Jacko?" Pat said.

"Aye, Jacko. Joe would want me to try and help him. But mainly I want us all to have some kind of ease in our lives. Most of all I want to see Brigid back at school, gettin' an education. That's what'll stand to her. And I want things to go well between Ned and Joe." She put her cup down, straightened her shoulders and said, "Do you know I'm suddenly not tired anymore? We'll drive on now with a firm and an easy mind."

"One mind between the three of us?" asked Brigid with a smile.

"Three minds with one purpose," said Maggie.

* * * * *

Noeleen Crowe had been very quiet since lunchtime. Even her father, who was usually too busy with his writing to notice such things, remarked on it to Mrs Grady.

Mrs Grady agreed."It's ever since she went

to visit the Murphys. She hardly said a word when she got back. I can't even get out of her if they're all coming to tea on Sunday. But I've decided to bake the cake anyway."

"Certainly it won't go to waste," Mr Crowe said.

"Oh, I know that. Now unless I'm very much mistaken that's Martin Delaney's van from Athlone with that book you've been waiting on. And I hope some of that special oatmeal for your wife."

Mrs Grady accepted the messages from Martin and as she closed the front door she called out,"Noeleen, will you come and give me a hand with this? Martin Delaney somehow managed to burst the bag of oatmeal. He wrapped a newspaper around it but it's spilling out onto the floor. Noeleen, did you hear me?"

"Yes, yes, I'm coming."

Mrs Grady was by the hall stand with Mr Crowe's book under one arm, and in her hands, the newspaper containing the torn bag of oatmeal. "Take it from me carefully now and leave it on the kitchen table." More oatmeal fell onto the floor as she transferred the parcel to Noeleen. "I'll hand the book into your Dad."

"It wouldn't have killed him to come out for it," Noeleen said before remembering her intention to seem good-natured to Mrs Grady. So she quickly added, "I suppose he's busy."

She put the parcel in the middle of the kitchen table and was about to go back to her silent consideration of how to find out what was happening over at the bungalow when she caught sight of the headline on the newspaper. "MISSING BOY SOUGHT IN IRELAND." There was a photograph too, of the boy she'd seen over at the Murphys'.

Quickly she took the oatmeal storage jar off the dresser and started to empty the contents of the torn bag into it.

Mrs Grady came in and watched her. "You're a constant source of amazement to me. You really are. One minute you'd rather die than help, then you do things without being asked."

"Turning over a new leaf isn't all that easy," Noeleen said. "Sometimes I just forget. What about this oatmeal in the newspaper? Will I throw it out for the birds?"

"Yes do, along with the stuff that got spilt in the hall."

Noeleen quickly scooped up the oatmeal off the floor and threw it into the frozen garden.

Then she went back to the sofa in the living room and read the newspaper.

"MISSING BOY SOUGHT IN IRELAND.

"The search for Joseph Mathews, the missing twelve year old boy, switched to the Republic to-day following reports that he had been seen on the night ferry from Liverpool.

"Mrs Annie Coughlan, passenger on the same boat, said 'I spoke to a boy who looked like the boy I saw in the English papers. He seemed to me to be travelling alone.'

"The staff at the Meehan Institute for Boys at Carringdon became concerned as to the boy's whereabouts when it was discovered that the address given to them by the boy's father was an accommodation address.

"Mr Lawford, the director of the Institute, said 'Joseph left the Institute, with our permission, for a brief holiday with his father. The possibility that he has been taken out of the country is most worrying.'"

"Well, well," thought Noeleen. "No wonder Bart and Kitty Murphy didn't want me to meet their cousin."

She examined the photograph carefull and once more read the report. Then, satisfied that she had all the details fixed in her mind, she rolled up the newspaper and put it under the turf and sticks in the fireplace. Her father would light the fire later on. He always insisted on a fire in the evenings in spite of the central heating. "There's nothing worse than a fireplace without a fire," he always said.

And there was nothing better than a secret uncovered, thought Noeleen.

She put on her overcoat and wellingtons, opened the front door and, making sure that Mrs Grady would not get from the kitchen in time to question her, said "I'm off for another walk."

The wind wasn't nearly as cold now. Most of the snow had vanished off the roads although it still lingered in sheltered corners and in the crevices and roofs of the Nuns' Chapel and the main buildings of Clonmacnoise. The information centre looked closed. But even as Noeleen decided this, the same car as had passed her on her previous visit to the bungalow cruised by.

There was still no wave or bleep on the horn as it pulled into the car park close to the main entrance of the ruins of the monastery. No one got out and Noeleen could just see the outlin of two figures in the car, one more than previously.

She walked on down the road, turned to the

left and then scrambled over the wall of the junior school whose mid-term break hadn't begun yet. The teacher and the pupils in the first classroom raised startled heads but Noeleen was too intent on keeping an eye on the car to bother about them.

She was soon out of sight of them anyway, dodging around the rear of the building and making for a hillock in a neighbouring field.

She was just in time to see the car drive off in the direction of Shannonbridge. Then just as quickly it turned and drove back down towards the ruins.

"Whoever is in it is looking for something or someone," Noeleen thought.

She heard another vehicle coming along the road from the direction of the bungalow. When it got to the high ridge on the road, Noeleen recognised it at once as Owen Murphy's car, on its way back after lunch.

The unfamiliar car by the ruins turned and slowly set off after the Murphys' car.

That was it then. The people in the car were looking for Owen Murphy. It was probably someone from The Meehan Institute for Boys!

Noeleen scrambled over a rickety wire fence and was soon within sight of the bungalow. In the yard behind it Bart was tending to a herd of cattle. He must have been on the look-out for visitors because he called out something to Kitty who at once came out to meet Noeleen.

Noeleen spoke first.

"How's your cousin now?"

"He's still resting."

"He must be very tired. But then it's a long way from England?"

"What makes you think he came from England?"

"His name is Joe Mathews. I read it in a newspaper.

The wind flicked Kitty's hair across her eyes. She pushed it back and looked hard at Noeleen.

"What is it?" Bart had finished with the cattle and hurried towards them.

"I was just asking how your cousin, Joe Mathews was. I'd like to meet him and the sooner the better."

"Wait here," Bart said.

He and Kitty ran to the bungalow. Their mother was in the living room working on a patchwork quilt.

"Noeleen Crowe is outside. She read about Joe in a newspaper," Kitty said. "She wants to meet him."

Mrs Murphy began to fold up her work.

"Are you going to let her into Joe's room?"

"There's not much point in keeping her out now but first I need to talk to her."

Noeleen found it difficult to be as hard with Mrs Murphy as she did with Kitty and Bart. After all she had no reason to dislike her.

"This newspaper that you read," Mrs Murphy began. "Where did you get it?"

"It came wrapped around a bag from Athlone."

"So your parents and Mrs Grady have seen it as well?"

"No, only me."

"But you told them?"

"No."

"Why not?"

"Because she thinks she can make us do whatever she likes by keeping it a secret," Kitty said.

"Well, if you'd told me in the first place everything would have been all right," replied Noeleen, "but you and Bart are always leaving me out of things. Even at school you never pick me to be on your side."

"We used to pick you all the time but you never wanted to play properly. You always wanted to be the boss and to change the rules to suit yourself," Bart said. "When we wouldn't let you do that you'd get into a huf and try to start trouble. That's why no one likes you."

"Well, you'd better start liking me now."

"Or you'd tell everyone about Joe?" Mrs Murphy was shocked. "You'd risk Joe's safety just so you can be the leader in the games at school?"

"It's not just school. It's everything. I'm always being left out, not that I can't get on without any of the stupid kids around here, if I wanted to."

"Then why don't you get on without us?" demanded Kitty.

"Children, please. You'll end up saying things you'll be sorry for," Mrs Murphy said.

"I won't," declared Noeleen, "because I know something that none of you do."

"You know something about Joe? Something more than was in the newspaper?"

"Yes."

"What, Noeleen? You must tell us. It could be very important." Noeleen had never heard anyone sound so serious as Mrs Murphy.

"I think the people from the Institute are after him," Noeleen said. "I saw a car driving around this morning. It followed me again just now. Then it drove off after Mr Murphy. I couldn't see who was in it."

"The people from the Meehan Insitute would come straight here," Mrs Murphy said.

"But who else would be looking for Joe?" Noeleen asked.

"Lots of people." Joe was standing at the door of the sitting room, a warm dressing gown over his pyjamas, Bart's slippers on his feet.

"You shouldn't be out of bed," Mrs Murphy said.

"I'm fine, Aunt Patricia," Joe said. "I'll be even better when I'm dressed only I wasn't sure if I should go on wearing Bart's clothes or if the ones I arrived in were all right for me to put back on."

"You can wear mine for as long as you like," said Bart.

"Thanks, Bart, but the ones I arrived in have to go back to the Mulligans in Dublin."

"In Dublin?" Mrs Murphy rose to her feet. "What are you talking about Dublin for?"

"It might not be safe for me to stay here now."

"Not safe? Where else could you be safer?" his aunt demanded.

"You don't know the Organiser," Joe said quietly. "It's his friends that are driving around looking for me."

"But how could they know where you are? Noeleen found out just by chance," Kitty said.

"That tinker woman in the caravan close to Tullamore saw me in the back of the car. She might have recognised your mother too."

"Why would a tinker woman recognise Mrs Murphy?" asked Noeleen.

"That's a story that will have to wait for another day," Mrs Murphy said firmly, "but it's not one that you can use for your own good."

"I didn't mean it like that at all," Noeleen said. "It's true that I was feeling cross and fed-up with Kitty and Bart. It's true that I came here to try and get the better of them but I didn't realise how serious things were until I saw ..." she glanced at Joe and then quickly glanced away, "until I saw Joe. I thought it was just a ... a kind of game."

Noeleen couldn't find the words she needed to tell the effect that Joe's appearance had had on her. He was quite different from the picture in the paper. He looked older and wiser and, in some strange way, very sad. He made Noeleen want to be his friend, part of the plan to help him.

"Well, now you know it's not a game. If only

the 'phone wasn't out of order we could get word to Owen," Mrs Murphy said.

"Our telephone is working," Noeleen said. "Maybe Bart could come over and use it. I won't say a word about Joe to my parents or to Mrs Grady if you don't want me to."

"I suppose that's the best idea," Mrs Murphy said.

"What do you want me to say to Dad?" Bart asked.

"Tell him that he'd best be careful of being followed. If we could even borrow another car ..."

"I'm sure Dad would lend him his. Mr Murphy could drive to our place and just change over." Noeleen hesitated, "Only he might have to explain why he needed a different car."

"He's going to have to explain soon or later," Mrs Murphy said "so he might as well start now."

"I'll get dressed just in case," Joe said.

Chapter 14

Into the Trap

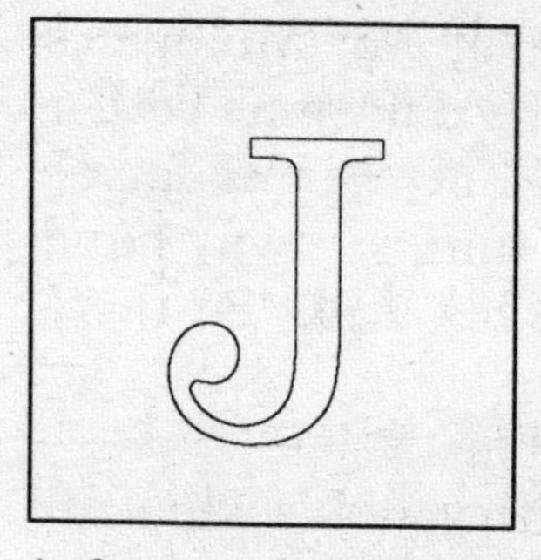

acko wandered through the city still undecided what to do with the information he'd got from Maisie.

He had no one to talk to, no one he could trust. He finally went back to Mrs Nolan's and ate the rest of the ham and cheese but that did nothing to solve his problem so he set out once more on his restless walking until he found himself outside the O'Connors' caravan close to the river Liffey.

Mrs O'Connor glared angrily at him. "Clear off from here, Jacko," she said. "You could have got my two little girls into terrible trouble doing the Organiser's dirty work. If you try the same thing again I'll let Mr Mulligan take care of you."

Mr Mulligan was the only person Jacko hadn't thought of, yet here was Mrs O'Connor talking of him as though he was more powerful than the Organiser! It was Mr Mulligan that Jacko would go to with the information about Joe being in Co. Offaly.

He knew the number of Mr Mulligan's house in Joyce Gardens. He'd have no bother finding it again but he'd only got as far as O'Connell Street when a thin, scrawny hand reached out and grasped his arm. "So there you are," Mollser said.

"What do you want with me?"

"It's not what I want with you. It's what our great friend wants with you."

"And who do you mean by that?"

Mollser lowered her voice to a whisper. "The Organiser, of course. Who did you think I meant?"

Jacko was stunned. He'd got used to the idea that the Organiser was no longer someone to be concerned with.

"Where is he?"

"I'll take you to him."

Mollser escorted Jacko down Henry Street and around the back of one of the great shops where a cleared space had been turned into a carpark. She pointed at a small black car. "He's in there."

The Organiser seemed to have something

wrong with the side of his face. It kept twitching. His eyes were grim and tired looking. There was no trace of the dangerous smile that Jacko always associated with him. Nor did the Organiser waste any time by trying to sound cheerful. "You let that lad from England get away the other evening."

"I couldn't help it," Jacko said.

"No, no one it seems can help anything that's been happening lately. I suppose you don't know where Mrs Nolan is?"

"I think she's gone away."

"And what about Sean?"

"I thought Sean was with you."

"Yes, until he drove off last night in my car leaving me stranded with that gang of tinkers. I think that he expected me to stay in the cinema forever. He seems to forget that there are such things as hired cars."

"Is this a hired car?"

"Yes, but if you're thinking of going back to report what kind of car it is you can forget that idea. I'm going to change it this afternoon. And tomorrow morning I'll have a third one and then a fourth and then, as many as I need, until I catch up with all those who've betrayed me. But maybe, Jacko, you're no longer on my side. Maybe you think I can no longer arrange for you to be sent to that brand new detention centre down the country."

"Joe says that you couldn't do that without getting yourself into trouble."

"Oh, so it's Joe who tells you what to do now is it? Did you hear that, Mollser?"

Mollser cocked her head to one side. "Aye, I did. And I'll tell you this much, this brat knows more than he's lettin' on. I was told that he was seen talkin' to Maisie, Sean's sister, this morning. It's the first I knew of them bein' on speakin' terms."

Jacko made as if to back away from the car but Mollser pushed him closer to it.

"So," the Organiser said, "you thought to join my enemies, did you? And don't lie. You know I can tell when you are lying." The Organiser shook Jacko slightly as he spoke and then pushed him hard against the front seat of the car. "What do you know about Sean and Mrs Nolan?"

"He and Mrs Nolan ..." Jack tried to sort his words out.

"Tell me!" The Organiser shook Jacko again and it was as though the car trembled at the big man's fury.

"After Joe got away from me the other night I went around to the vegetable shop. Sean was there with Mrs Nolan."

"What was said?"

"We talked about Joe and how we had to get him back."

"Nothing else? Nothing about money or a list?"

"No, nothing."

"It could have been all said, all fixed before Jacko got there," Mollser said.

"Maybe." The Organiser turned his attention back to Jacko. "What did Sean's sister say to you this morning?"

"Something about the people in the pub in Carroll's Bridge going off."

"So they are all in it," the Organiser said.

"What about the money you mentioned? And the list? " Mollser asked the Organiser. "What kind of list?"

"A list of names. Oh don't worry. You're not on it, Mollser. Neither is Jacko. Neither am I." There was a kind of confidence returning to the Organiser now. "But it's the money I'm concerned about now. And I'm speaking of real money, thousands of pounds, that I need to get my hands on so that I can vanish for a while."

"Have you got it hidden somewhere?" Mollser asked eagerly.

The Organiser laughed for the first time

since returning to the city. "And do you think I'd be foolish enough to tell you where?"

Mollser tried to look innocent. "I just meant that if you did have it hid maybe one of us could go and get it for you."

"I'm doing my own collecting from this time on," the Organiser said, "although Jacko might lend a hand in a very small matter that would bring me nearer to having that money. You'll help, won't you, Jacko?"

Jacko nodded.

"There's a bunch of keys hidden in the garden of the house where our last meeting was. You remember the statue of the lion?"

Jacko nodded again.

"The keys are under the ivy that's growing over it. Bring them back here to me. Not a word to anyone."

"All right." Jacko wriggled out of the car and set off down the side street.

"Were you wise to trust him?" Maggie asked. "I could have just as easy gone for them."

"You'd take too long. Besides I've other work for you. Find out who else Sean's sister spoke to this morning."

"Well, I can tell you one person and that was Jenny O'Shea."

"Do I know this Jenny O'Shea?"

"She helped once or twice but she wasn't much good, forever goin' back to Co. Offaly."

"Co. Offaly, eh?"

"You don't think that's where Joe is?"

"Why not?"

"You still need to find him then?"

"Oh yes, I do, Mollser, if only to teach him and his father a lesson, which is that they can't make a fool of me. That's the kind of lesson I'm about to teach Sean and Mrs Nolan and the others too."

"Well let me assure you that it's not the kind of lesson you'll ever have cause to teach me."

"I'm glad to hear that, Mollser, because the greatest mistake anyone could make now is to imagine that I am beaten. Now off you go and find out what this Jenny O'Shea told Sean's sister."

"Will you be safe here though?"

"What place could be safer than a public carpark in the middle of the city?"

"What if Jacko doesn't bring the keys back?"

"It is possible to have more than one set of keys."

"It's a test then that you've given him to see if he's to be trusted?"

"Exactly, Mollser, just as I suppose you

could say that the task I've given you is a kind of test."

Mollser set off in the same direction as Jacko. The Organiser watched her through half-closed eyes. He wished he'd encouraged his followers to call him 'sir'. Maybe he would when he'd finally fixed those who had turned against him. He smiled as he thought of Mrs Nolan and Sean trying to find the list down in Oakfield House.

* * * * *

It was colder inside Oakfield House than it was outside.

Sean rubbed his hands briskly together. "Do you think Mick O'Donoghue recognised us?"

"I don't see how he could fail to recognise you" Mrs Nolan said. "If I don't get out of here soon I won't be able to walk. My feet are frozen."

"Put on dry shoes and stockings then. Will I get you some out of the case?"

Mrs Nolan grabbed her suitcase. "No. It's all right. Let's get on with finding the list."

"The suitcase is not goin' to run away, you know," Sean said thoughtfully.

"I might forget it."

"Fat chance of that happening. I suppose you still want me to carry it for you."

"No, I can manage. Just show me the room."

Sean climbed the stairs with Mrs Nolan a few inches behind him. He opened the door of the room with the folded blankets.

"No one's been in here. You can tell that by the dust. Only I'd like to get my hands on whoever flung my stuff around. Hey, it wasn't you, was it? Were you here before now lookin' for the list?"

"Oh, don't keep wasting time." Mrs Nolan pushed past him into the room. "Where is the list hidden?" She tightened her grip on the suitcase.

"Let me see what you have in the suitcase first."

"You must be mad if you think I'm going to open my case in this filthy room. There's only one place the list could be." She moved towards the bed but Sean got there first, snatching the blankets out of her reach. "Not so fast," he began to say as the envelope slid into view.

"How slow you are!" Mrs Nolan seized the envelope with her free hand and started back down the stairs.

"Come back!" Sean dropped the blankets

and raced after her.

Mrs Nolan had reached the font door and might have got as far as the gate if at that moment two men, that neither of them had seen before, hadn't stepped into the hall. "Mrs Nolan?" one of them asked. "The owner of this house?"

Mrs Nolan hesitated.

The second one looked at Sean. "And this is the man who caretakes this house for you?"

"You'll have to excuse me. I'm in a hurry." Mrs Nolan made as if to push past the men but the one who had spoken first removed the envelope from her grasp. "That is a private letter," Mrs Nolan said.

"It doesn't seem to be addressed to anyone. In fact it seems to have been opened and stuck again with tape. By the way, I'm Inspector Doyle. This is Detective Regan." Inspector Doyle opened the letter and drew out the folded supermarket bag. He looked at Mrs Nolan and then at Sean. "I take it that this is not what you expected to find in the envelope. I take it it might be more like a list of names. Now what about this suitcase?"

"Personal things," Mrs Nolan said "Clothes."

"Heavy clothes by the way you are holding

it." He took the case very gently from Mrs Nolan. "With your permission?" He flicked the locks open and lifted the lid. It was full of ten pound notes. "I hope for both your sakes that these are genuine banknotes."

"It had nothing to do with me, nothing." Sean came sorrowfully downstairs. "I'm just employed to look after the place here, sir. It's all a terrible mistake."

"Yes, on your part."

"I know nothing about the money in the suitcase. You've only my word against hers and that gang of tinkers, the O'Donoghues, betraying one of their own."

"Our information didn't come from the tinkers. It came from a telephone box in Dublin. A man's voice, very distinctive. He also spoke of a stolen car."

"The Organiser!" Sean said. "But how did he know we'd be here?"

"Be quiet," Mrs Nolan snapped. "You've said too much already."

"And small wonder if I have after all the risks I've taken, trudging through the snow, being made a laughing stock of."

"You walked here then, did you?" the Inspector asked.

"Part of the way."

The Inspector consulted a notebook and read out the number of the Organiser's car. "We had another telephone call in connection with this car. It came from a farmer and his wife, who gave bed and breakfast to a man last night. They didn't care much for the look of him. The car was found by another farmer in a field when he went out to tend to his livestock. It looked as though it had been in an accident. You were driving that car. Did you have the owner's permission or did you steal it?"

Sean lapsed into silence. There was no point in denying the charge.

"And now about your car, Mrs Nolan? Your car was found further along the road. It was the worse for wear as well. Another accident? Or the same one as your caretaker was involved in?"

"The cars skidded. We had to leave them," Mrs Nolan said.

"In order to get here and collect a list of names? You see, we have been keeping a close eye on all that's been happening. We'd have known you were here even without the phone call from this so-called Organiser. We know his real name, of course, from his being questioned the other night. Your friends from the pub in Carroll's Bridge were also victims of the weather."

Mrs Nolan's eyes widened. "They had an accident as well?"

"More a hold-up than an accident. The snow storm closed the airport. We have a search warrant for the pub. Now about this money. Is it yours?"

Mrs Nolan shook her head. "No. It belongs to the Organiser."

Sean was terrified by her words. "You stole the Organiser's money? How did you get your hands on it?"

Mrs Nolan sighed. "I watched. I listened. I stayed quiet. I had my spies follow the Organiser and find out where he lived. Then on the night that Joe got away from us the Organiser stopped at the statue of the lion in the garden. He pretended he was tying his shoe-lace but I saw him drop a bunch of keys. He didn't want them to be found on him."

"What did the keys open?" the Inspector asked.

"They opened the door of a flat and inside that flat there was a safe. The money was there." She shivered. "I presume you want us to go with you. I hope you've got proper heating in your car."

"We'll do our best," the Inspector said.

Mrs Nolan paused on the doorstep and looked back into the house. "To think that it all started because of this place. I had a plan to turn it into a hotel overlooking the Liffey with plenty of good fishing and horse riding. But I got greedy and became as bad as the Organiser. Isn't there a saying about having supper with the devil?"

"Yes. When you sup with the devil use a long spoon."

"My spoon wasn't long enough." Mrs Nolan managed a smile. "We were all following each other, spying on each other, planning to betray each other. And one boy and his father, who had no notion of what was going on, ruined it all."

"You must tell us all about this lad and his father," the Inspector said.

* * * * *

Bart came back into the Crowes' living room where Mr Crowe and Noeleen sat, waiting. "My father says he'll come over as soon as he can and swop cars with you. I think I'd better go on home and let Mam know that I got through all right."

"Will you not wait for your father?" Mr

Crowe asked.

"He doesn't know how long he'll be. He can't just walk off the job at a moment's notice."

Noeleen said, "Do you want me to come back with you?"

"No, thanks. I mean, there's nothing you could do."

Mr Crowe said, "Noeleen knows how you meant it. Don't worry."

Noeleen nodded in agreement. She felt that there was a good chance that she and the Murphys would become good friends.

Chapter 15
Final Moves

he pavements in Joyce Gardens had been swept clear of snow. Neat piles of it lined the gutter. A cat walked daintily across a front garden, lifting her paws high in the air with every step. She paused momentarily like a marmalade statue as Jacko ran to the front door of number twelve and pressed the bell.

Mr Mulligan opened the door and recognised the young boy. "You're Jacko, aren't you? Have you news?"

"They know that Joe's in Offaly."

"Who knows?"

"Sean's sister and some other people. They have the number of the car. But when you take over from the the Organiser will you remember that I helped Joe?"

"I'm not going to take over from the

Organiser," Mr Mulligan said.

"Then who is? Joe's Da?"

"No one is."

"No one?"

"The Organiser is finished. The guards have a list of names."

"Who's that?" Mrs Mulligan came out of the kitchen.

"It's Jacko come with a message."

Mrs Mulligan looked at the frightened child. Jacko backed away.

"Hold on a second," Mr Mulligan said.

"I can't." Jacko left the garden gate bouncing on its hinges with the force with which he pushed it.

The Organiser was still in control. Jacko would have to take a bus if he was to make up for the time he had wasted.

He jumped on the first one that passed him. Soon he jumped off that and onto another. He was Jacko, King of the Trail again, only he was headed west on green buses instead of in covered wagons!

* * * * *

Joe and Kitty looked out the window of the sitting room. The weather had suddenly improved. County Galway on the other side of the river sparkled in the clear sunshine. A car drove across the cattle grid.

"Whose car is that?"

"Mr Crowe's! Dad did the swap! I'll let him and Bart in!"

But only Owen Murphy got out of the car.

"Where's Bart?" Kitty asked. "Did he stay over at the Crowes?"

"No. He left before I got there. He should be home by now."

"Well, he isn't."

Mrs Murphy turned very pale when she heard Bart was not with his father.

Owen said, "He maybe took a short cut across the field and had to turn back because of the state of the ground."

"Or the bog," Katie said. "He thought we saw lights on the bog a few nights ago. Maybe Bart saw something else when he left the Crowes' and went to investigate."

"He'd never be that foolish," Mrs Murphy said "and yet with all the excitement he might not have stopped to think. If he decided that it was important ..."

Owen interrupted his wife and spoke to his daughter. "Kitty, can you point out where Mr Crowe saw these lights?"

"Yes, it was near where turf was cut last summer by the Costelloes."

"Put on your wellingtons and show me exactly. Joe, you stay here with your aunt. No matter what, don't move until we come back."

Mrs Murphy didn't speak a word as Kitty got ready and drove off with her father. Finally Joe could stand the silence no longer. "You think something has happened to Bart, don't you?"

"I just couldn't help thinking that at a distance he might be mistaken for you. Oh, I'm sorry. That sounds as though I'm blaming you."

"No, Aunt Patricia. You really think that whoever has been looking for me has him. You were afraid to say it out loud in case that somehow made it come true."

Aunt Patricia could not deny this. "But I'm sure that when they realise that they've made a mistake they'll let Bart go."

"There's only one way they will let Bart go and that is if they get me instead."

"What on earth are you thinking of doing, Joe?" Aunt Patricia looked at Joe's determined face.

"Just letting them see that I'm here."

"You'll can't do that. You've been very ill."

"I won't go very far," Joe said.

"You'll go nowhere at all except straight in and sit beside the fire."

The telephone suddenly tinkled.

Aunt Patricia rushed to it. "Hello? Hello?"

There was no voice at the other end.

"They must be just repairing the lines now." Aunt Patricia came back into the hall. "That was the tinkle we heard …"

But she was talking to herself. Joe was gone.

Aunt Patricia made to run after him and then realised that she had her oldest slippers on. She'd get nowhere in those. "Oh Joe," she said as she scrambled about in the hall closet for her wellingtons. "Joe, don't undo all the good work of the last few days."

But Joe had no such idea in his head. He really had no plan at all except to get to the high point on the road from where he could easily be seen. He heard a vehicle down on the main road.

Joe ran toward the sound as a van rattled around the corner. Then he stood still, thinking for an instant that he was imagining things as the van stopped and Brigid and Maggie and Pat got out of it.

"You're all right?" Maggie asked.

"Yes, but Bart's gone. We think he might have been taken in mistake for me."

"We passed nothing on the road from Moate, not a thing."

"What about the other direction? Joe asked "My cousins mentioned a place called Shannonbridge."

"We'll try there, only what kind of car are we looking for?" Pat asked as they all piled back into the van.

"I'm not sure," Joe said. "A girl called Noeleen Crowe knows but I don't know where she lives."

"Then it's worse than useless. We can't go charging up to every car we meet," Pat said.

"Neither can we just sit here," said Maggie.

"What's that?" Brigid climbed back out of the van. "I heard someone shouting."

"Kitty and her father are down on the bog. Could it be them? We can see from further back there."

"No, that's not where I heard the voice coming from. Look!"

Noeleen Crowe was scrambling over a fence, her hair streaming out behind her.

"The monastery," she yelled. "The car is down by the monastery." She had almost reached the van now. "I was coming over with more comics when I saw the car." She suddenly noticed that her hands were empty. "I seem to have dropped them. But never mind that."

"Go to the bungalow and tell Mrs Murphy," Maggie said. "Away with us, Pat!"

"Hey, hold on," Brigid yelled but Pat had already driven off, forgetting that his sister was not in the van.

"Come in," Noeleen said "We have work to do."

The van seemed to slide down towards the ruined buildings. Smoke trickled from the chimney of the house next to the Information Centre. A faint sound of children singing came from the school.

Joe got out of the van and walked towards the parked car. He could hear Pat and Maggie following him.

The driver's door opened. A man got out. "So it seems we made a bit of a mistake." He glanced at the newspaper in his hand. "But the photo is a bit old, I'd wager."

"That's not all I'd wager," Maggie said quietly. "I'd wager you made more than a bit of a mistake, Patch O'Shea."

"Is that so, Maggie? We haven't met this long time."

"Where's Bart?" Joe asked.

"In the car with my brother, Christy."

"Let him go and I'll come with you instead," Joe said.

Patch laughed. "And have every guard in the country after us within five minutes? No, thanks. As soon as I realised we had the wrong lad we knew as well that this game wasn't our kind of game at all. Christy, let the lad out."

Bart looked none the worst for his experience.

"You're being very sensible," Maggie said to Patch. "But what caused you to get mixed up in this business in the first place?"

"It seemed like a good idea. We knew the Organiser and Sean and his lot were looking for the lad from England. We thought he might as well come along with us as stay with the Murphys up beyond. We thought there might be a bit of money in it for us eventually. What connection is there between Joe Mathews and the Murphys anyway?"

"None of that need concern you," Maggie said.

"Nor will it if what happens here can be regarded as a mistake on our part," Patch said.

Maggie said "I make no promises on that.

That would depend on how closely connected you are with the Organiser."

"Not closely connected at all so far."

"You'd best keep it that way."

Patch nodded in agreement, got into his car and drove out of the car-park.

"Where's Brigid?" Pat suddenly noticed that his sister wasn't with them.

"Back there with Noeleen," Joe said, "or more likely on her way here with Aunt Patricia."

"Then we'd best move and save them some of the walk," Pat said.

"How did they get you into the car?" Joe asked Bart as they settled in the back of the van.

"They just pulled up beside me and grabbed hold of me. But I wasn't really frightened. I knew Dad or someone would come after me."

"Your Dad and Kitty went to see if you were on the bog."

Maggie laughed. "Well, no doubt but it's great to have energy. I'm Maggie. This is Pat O'Donoghue. His father and me knew your mother years ago."

"When she was growing up in Galway?"

"You know about that then? Good. There's your mother now and the two girls."

Aunt Patricia leaned in through the open window. "Oh, Maggie, it's you. Are the boys all right? They'll be the death of me yet! They really will!"

"The making of you is more likely for these are two grand lads. And I'm looking forward to meeting your daughter."

"And my husband too, I hope. That is if they haven't sunk in the bog. Bart, would you go and let them know you're all right?"

"I'm certain this is the place where Mr Crowe saw the lights," Kitty said. She squelched forward a few more inches.

"Well there seems to be nothing here," her father said, "or if there was it's gone now. But hold on a second. Look over there at that stook of turf. Someone's been moving around there recently." He carefully moved towards the carefully built pile. "Do you see where something has been dragged along and there's a cigarette butt in the corner there? I'm going around the other side."

Brigid followed him, making sure to step exactly where he had stepped. They stared at what looked like an entrance into the turf pile.

"It's almost as though someone was using it as a house," Brigid said.

"Or stealing the turf from the inside so that anyone looking at it from the road wouldn't notice anything odd about it."

"Poor Mr Crowe," Kitty said "he was hoping it was flying saucers. Instead it's just someone helping themselves to the Costelloes' turf! But there's no sign that Bart has been here."

"No, no sign at all. We'd best get back." Owen held his hand out to his daughter and they picked their way carefully back to solid ground. "Only if he's not here then where is he?"

Suddenly a great smile crossed Kitty's face. "He's over there," she said, "along with Joe and Noeleen and a girl I never saw before." She ran forward to meet them. "Are you all all right?"

"We're great. You missed right excitement. But what did you and Dad find there?" Bart asked.

"Cigarette butts and turf stealing," Kitty replied.

The others were very disappointed.

"So those lights had nothing to do with Joe or with travellers from space?" Bart said.

"Maybe it's travellers from space you want

along with everything else," his father declared.

"I was thinking of Mr Crowe and the book he's writing," Bart said.

"Oh don't worry about Dad," Noeleen said. "He'll use his imaginations."

"All the same it would be great if it was true," Bart sighed.

* * * * *

The ivy around the statue of the lion was frozen so hard that it seemed as hard as metal when Jacko touched it. He moved his fingers carefully around and through and under its leaves but there as no bunch of keys to be found.

He examined the ground in case the keys had somehow ended up there. But, no, there were definitely no keys anywhere. Could the Organiser have made a mistake? The Organiser had been making mistakes, lots of mistakes, lately. Jacko remembered the last time he'd been in this garden with Joe.

It had all ended with a great scattering of people and with Joe being taken back to Carroll's Bridge and Maggie.

Maggie had said she didn't use magic. Yet

everything seemed to lead back to her. She knew everything about everyone from Joe to Sean to Mrs Nolan. She might even know that the Organiser was sitting waiting in his hired car in that car park.

It was to her he should have gone , not to Mr Mulligan. But how was he to get to Carroll's Bridge? Where could he shelter if he did not go back and tell the Organiser that his keys were gone?

Then a smile crept across the boy's face as he remembered he had another set of keys; the keys to Mrs Nolan's shop. Jacko Maguire, King of the Trail, would be safe there.

* * * * *

Noeleen Crowe sat silently in a corner of the Murphys' kitchen and watched as Mrs Murphy and Kitty and Brigid set the table and got food ready. Maggie had been told to stay and get warm by the fire next to Joe, who certainly looked none the worse for having been out in the cold.

Bart and his father were in the yard tending to the livestock. The gentle lowing of the cattle was strangely comforting. They had been silent all morning. Now it was as though they were reassuring the world that everything was all right.

Certainly anyone looking into the kitchen would never realise that so much had happened in so short a time.

Maggie and Mrs Murphy became aware then at the same time of Noeleen, sitting so quietly in the corner.

Maggie said, "I can almost hear the question goin' around inside the young girl's head."

"So can I," Mrs Murphy agreed.

"It's a long tale if it has to be told," Maggie said.

"Oh, you don't have to tell me anything," Noeleen said. "It's none of my business and anyway ..."

"Anyway what?" Maggie asked.

"Well, Bart and Kitty don't really like me. I don't blame them for that. I've been horrid to them. Not because I didn't like them or want to be friends with them. It's just that I didn't like living here with my mother sick in bed and Dad always busy with his writing. I mean Kitty and Bart might not want me to know their secrets."

"You said you *didn't* like living here. Does that mean you *do* like living here now?"

"I liked being here this morning with all the excitement."

"And you certainly did help," Mrs Murphy said. "You saved Bart and Joe when you saw the car by the ruins. As for secrets, Kitty and Bart and Joe will have to make their own minds up as to what they do or do not tell you."

"I know that people in England are looking for Joe," Noeleen said.

"Joe did nothing wrong," Kitty said.

"And he is also well able to talk for himself," her mother reminded her.

"I was just thinking of where we all stand," Joe said. "I think that I might really be safe here now. It might be the beginning of a new pattern for me. I only wish I knew where my father was."

The telephone blared into life, its ringing seeming louder than a hundred church bells.

"It's fixed," Mrs Murphy said. "It tinkled a while ago but now it's fixed."

"Should we not answer it?" Maggie suggested.

"Of course."

But Owen and Bart had already come rushing in from the yard, trailing soft muck across the floor. "Leave it to me," Owen said, lifting the receiver. "Hello ... Ned! I don't believe it. Well, there was a bit of a drama just now ... No, he's fine. Here, let me put him onto you."

Joe took the receiver from his uncle. "Hello, Dad? I mean Ned."

"Oh, it's all right. You can call me Dad if you want. You can call me anything you like. I've been trying to get through since last night."

"The phone was out of order."

"Yes, so they told me."

"Where are you?"

"In Carringdon."

"Carringdon? What are you doing there?"

"I came back to see Mr Lawford at the Institute. Joe? Are you still there, Joe?"

For a moment Joe had been taken back to Ned's last visit to the Institute. Had there been another row between Ned and Mr Lawford? "Oh yes, Dad. I'm still here. What happened? What did Mr Lawford say?"

"Well," Ned admitted, "he wasn't exactly pleased that I'd taken you to Ireland, even less pleased when I told him what had happened."

"You told him everything? About the Organiser? Everything?"

"Yes. I made a vow, remember, that from now on everything would be on the up-and-up."

"And what did Mr Lawford say to that?"

"He agreed that that was the only thing to do. He also agreed that for the moment you might be best left with your aunt and uncle."

Joe gave a cry of delight.

Now, now, hold on a second. 'For the moment' means for the next week or so until things cool off and until I get finished with some business."

"Business?" Joe felt a stab of fear.

"Oops," said Ned. "Sorry. Wrong choice of words. This time it's real business, not like the monkey business that brought me to Ireland. This business has to with my music. But I won't say anything more about that now. Just keep telling yourself that things are going to be all right. Remember that you are the most important person in the world as far as I'm concerned. Now let me have a word with your aunt."

It ended up with everyone, even Noeleen, speaking to Ned until finally Aunt Patricia said "This call must be costing him a fortune. Joe, you'd better say 'good-bye'."

"Hello, Dad. It's me again. When am I going to see you?"

"As soon as I can, you can rely on that."

"O.K 'Bye Dad."

"Good-bye, Joe."

Joe had never felt so happy. In fact he hated to put the receiver back down in case that somehow changed the way he felt. But at last he did so and looked at the smiling faces that surrounded him. "He'll be here as soon as he can make it."

"And that means you have to be one-hundred-per-cent fit," Aunt Patricia said.

"Don't worry," said Joe. "I will be."

* * * * *

The Organiser had a terrible pain in his right shoulder. The car wasn't really big enough for him to get more comfortable. It was over an hour since he'd sent Mollser to find Sean's sister and Jacko to find the keys. He'd have to face the fact that neither of them were coming back. They had deserted him like all the others.

He paid the parking fee to the attendant and drove down the side-street. There were two uniformed gardai standing in a doorway. They looked at him as he passed.

"Steady now," the Organiser said to himself. "Don't start imagining things."

He went straight to the newsagent around

the corner from the house where his flat was. He smiled as he went in. "Hello. Enjoying the cold weather? I seem to have mislaid my keys again. Do you still have the set I left with you?"

"I do, of course." The woman smiled back. She thought the Organiser was a grand man.

"Thanks."

The Organiser let himself into the house and up the stairs to the flat. As soon as he opened the door he knew that someone had been there before him. He was always very particular about how he left things.

He went into the bedroom. There were signs there as well of someone searching for something. The mirror in front of the safe wasn't straight. He took the mirror down and opened the safe. It was empty.

A voice behind him said, "If you're looking for the money, Mrs Nolan says she borrowed it."

The Organiser swung around. Inspector Doyle and Detective Regan were standing in the doorway. Inspector Doyle held up a bunch of keys. "We used these to get in. Mrs Nolan gave them to us. We have the list of the names as well. I think you'd better come along with us."

Chapter 16

Music in Galway

While most of the country shivered under icy conditions and the news was filled with reports of food having to be dropped by helicopter to isolated farms and communities, the area around Clonmacnoise seemed to enjoy an early thaw.

Maggie and the O'Donoghues had refused the Murphys' invitation to stay overnight and had set off for Carroll's Bridge.

Kitty and Bart and Noeleen were allowed to show Joe around on condition that he was well wrapped up and didn't stay longer than half-an-hour at a time.

He was delighted with the area. He soon knew as much as his cousins about the monastic ruins and the part they had played in Irish history. He was told too about the watermeadows that flooded during winter and during the spring and summer had a great blooming of wild flowers and grasses. Then there was the bog where a narrow railway line ran to help bring the great supplies of machine-cut turf to the loading places.

One day Aunt Patricia drove them into Shannonbridge and Joe saw the amazing fortifications that had been built in case Napoleon sailed up the river Shannon.

"And that's our school," Kitty said, pointing to a fine looking building.

"It looks great," Joe said.

"It is. It's a terrific school although I don't think Noeleen likes it very much."

"I think I've changed my mind about that," Noeleen said. "I feel more at home here now. I suppose I was a bit like Joe, not knowing where I belonged."

"What made you decide that you belonged here?" Bart asked.

"I just decided to try and enjoy things. I know it'd be a help to Mrs Grady and to my parents. Mind you," Noeleen added with a grin, "that doesn't mean I'm going to be a good-goody for ever and ever."

Bart grinned back. "We didn't think you meant that."

On Sunday afternoon Joe and the Murphys went to tea at the Crowes'. Mr Crowe was so interested in Joe's story that he almost forgot to talk to Owen about converting the outhouses. "If I ever get the time I might have a go at seeing if it would make a book. Or better again, Joe, why don't you try writing it down yourself?"

Joe had never thought of trying to write about anything that had happened to him and he told himself that Mr Crowe was just being polite when he made the suggestion. Yet when the school break was over and Joe was left on his own for most of the day he began to think more and more about what Mr Crowe had said.

He decided to talk it over with Aunt Patricia.

"I think it's a great idea," she said. "There's a notebook on top of the dresser that you can use. The place will be a hive of activity, you writing a book, me making that new quilt for Mrs Crowe."

"Mrs Crowe is a nice woman, isn't she?" Joe said.

"Most people are nice," his aunt replied. "The longer I live the more I realise that."

"Even the Organiser?"

"Well no, maybe not him or at least not yet. Don't forget that people can change."

"I wonder if Jacko can change. I wonder what's happened to him. Do you think Brigid or Maggie might know? Before I start writing the story maybe I should write to them, only what address would I put on it?"

"Why not send it care of the Post Office in Carroll's Bridge? Put your own name and this address on the back of the envelope. Then if it isn't delivered it'll come back here."

Joe wrote the letter at once and addressed it to Maggie. Then he settled into what was to be his routine for the next week, scribbling in the notebook, helping his aunt around the house and the yard and going to meet Kitty and Bart off the school bus.

Noeleen often came up the bungalow for tea and to play "sevens".

She told them that her father didn't believe that those lights on the bog were just someone stealing turf. "He says that he still sees them even though the Costelloes are keeping an eye out for the thief."

Exactly one week after he'd posted the letter to Maggie, Joe got a reply from her, written by Brigid.

"Dear Joe,

"The postman very kindly brought your letter out to me. Everything was grand at the camp when we got back. We are managing to keep reasonably warm and the snow, thank God, has all but vanished.

"There's no sign of anyone at Oakfield House. The rumours from Dublin are that the Organiser and his crowd have all been arrested. We were half-afraid to believe this when what do you think? The very person you wrote to me about turned up at the camp. Yes, Joe, it is to Jacko that I am referring. The very day after your letter came I heard Dingo and the other dogs kicking up a terrible row. And there was Jacko outside my caravan. He'd been hiding in Mrs Nolan's shop. He came by himself on the bus. Where the money came from I'm not sure. I'll find that out later. I'm hoping too to find out where his parents are. Until then he'll stay with me. Brigid and all your friends here send you their best. Don't forget us, God bless you, Maggie."

"Well now, that should set your mind at rest," Aunt Patricia said.

"It does. Now all we want is word from Ned, I mean Dad."

"And that will come when the time is right.

I'll bet in fact that you'll have heard from him before you've learned to milk the cow."

"Are you going to show me how to do that?"

"I am, of course. We'll turn you into a real farmer yet."

A real farmer? Joe had never thought of becoming a farmer. But then he'd never thought of writing a book either or that he'd learn so much about Irish history and the ruins of Clonmacnoise. He suddenly had so many things to choose from.

Milking the cow was not as easy as his aunt made it seem. The bucket got kicked over. Joe had his face slapped several times by a swishing tail. "I'll never get the hang of it."

Then quite unexpectedly he did get it right. Foaming milk began to fill the bucket. "Hey, look, Aunt Patricia!" he called out.

"That's perfect, just perfect," his aunt said. Then tilting her head "Is that the 'phone?"

"Ned!" Joe said. "It just has to be my dad!"

Joe reached the phone in record time. "I knew it was you. I just knew it."

"Well, I wonder what else you can tell."

"Do you mean like Maggie with the cards?"

"Or maybe just a guess."

"Well, that you are coming back to Ireland."

"That's right. I'm arriving at Shannon on

Ned

Tuesday morning, hiring a car and driving up to see you."

"That's great," Joe said.

"There's more," Ned said. "I've just made a demo disc."

"A record?"

"Yes. One of the recording companies thinks it has a good chance of doing well."

"Oh that's great, just great. What songs do you sing?"

"One new one that I wrote myself. One old one that your mother used to sing to you."

"Do you mean the lullaby?"

"Yes, Joe, I do."

It was almost lunch time when Ned arrived at the bungalow. Kitty and Bart had been allowed to take the day off school in order to welcome him.

They were very impressed by him and Joe was very proud.

Ned looked well, and happy and confident. He talked easily to them all and especially to Patricia.

When all the news had been exchanged Owen said, "I hope you can stay a while with us."

"I can if you'll have me. In fact my agent wants me to play in Galway next Friday. It's in one of the hotels, a charity cabaret. He thinks it'd be a good place to try out the songs. And I know Joe wants to visit Galway."

"He's already been there," Kitty said.

"To Galway?" Joe asked. "When?"

"When you crossed the river at Shannonbridge to look at the fortifications. The fortifications are on the Galway side of the river."

"That doesn't really count. That's County Galway." Joe said. "It's Friday's visit that's important."

There are some days that are never forgotten.

The Friday that Joe spent in Galway with Ned and the Murphys was one of those days for him.

They drove to the places where his aunt and his mother had lived. They visited the grave where his grandparents were buried. All his doubts and worries seemed to become unimportant. He knew who he was now.

And the cabaret in the hotel was the perfect end to the day. It was held in the ballroom which was crowded with people.

Kitty and Bart and Joe had to stay backstage and watch Ned perform. He sang other composers' songs first and got a good round of applause.

Then he started to sing the lullaby.

"The road is long
It slowly winds
To the house we know
So well..."

There wasn't another sound to be heard. It was as though everyone listening could take his own meaning from the words. Joe felt as though he understood them for the first time. He wished Brigid could hear them too and remind Maggie about The Thatched Barge and the idea of living there.

The lullaby finished. There was silence. Before that silence could be broken Ned struck a new set of chords on his guitar and suddenly the mood was changed as he sang his own new song.

"I've got the detained for questioning blues.
I couldn't go home if I choose.
They've closed the doors
They've locked the locks
Next thing they'll have me out breakin' up rocks ..."

By the time Ned got around to repeating

the first verse the audience were clapping and swaying in time to the music. Some of them even joined in the words.

Joe thought, "I know where he got the idea for that song. It must have been when he was being questioned by the guards."

The song finished. Cheers echoed around the ballroom. Ned walked off the stage. Sweat was pouring off his face. He gave Joe a hug. "Those songs are dedicated to you."

Then he went back onto the stage and began to play "Detained for Questioning Blues" all over again.

Joe crossed his fingers. If the recording was half as good as the performance maybe Ned's dream of being a famous musician would come true at long last.